Dead Man Standing

Voll Greene

Acknowledgements

First and foremost, I thank God for all that I've been through. Many days were tough, but if it were not for those times, I wouldn't be where I am now. Spiritual peace is priceless. I thank my mother and father and my brothers and sisters for never giving up on me. Gloria Miller, Marian & Voll Greene III, Evelynn & Voll Greene Jr; Walter Greene, William Greene, Cheryl Greene, Rusty Greene, Kevin Greene, Promise Greene & Lil Promise Greene, Estrada aka Hope Dadzie, Carrington Greene, Ruth Greene, Earnest Henry, Maria Harvey, Richard Henry, Paul Greene, Louis Harvey, Forest Harvey, La'Jacqulyn Smith, Andy Greene, Phong Greene, Noomi Greene, Elijah Greene, Bernice Miller, Linda Miller Crook,   Vernon Miller, Woody Miller, Handsome Miller, Princess Miller, Kayla Lymon, April Ameer, Brad Gardner, Shimeka Gardner, Tyra Greene, SheKeera Greene, Shikema Greene, Voll Greene Jr, Trevon Sams, Nirayl Dadzie, Kemiera Thurston, Wilmot Dadzie, Forest Harvey, Javarius Harvey, Tabius Harvey, Foreon Harvey, D. Mack the Author, Scinita, Nikki Turner, Joseph & Yusef Robinson, extended family members, friends, Local 2426, and so many others who I can't think to name at this moment that have touch my life. You all are greatly appreciated.

Chapter One

Thunder erupts as the lightning flashes across the sky. The storm is directly above the city. The streets are empty. A few people are running across the street. They're running to the only lounge that is open. As soon as they reach the door of the bar, the night sky is illuminated with a silvery- white glow, and it's followed with a powerful crackling sound – boom! The lightning strikes a power line. Sparks and flares of electricity are fluttering wildly. All of the street lights go out.

Inside the lounge, it's suddenly quiet. The whole building shook when the lightning hit its target. It scared everyone except for four friends, who are sitting at a table in the rear. All four of them seem to be oblivious to the thunderstorm outside.

"More drinks!" they shout.

The friends have been in the lounge for over three hours. They came for the happy hour at five o'clock and have been sitting in their places ever since.

Rell pats the air with his hand. "Guys, I think we need to tone it down just a notch."

Phillip quickly retorts, "Wait, who said 'It's Friday and we need to go somewhere where we can find some peace and relaxation?'"

"Hold up", Rell responds with noticeable frustration, "I know – that's exactly what I said, PEACE and RELAXATION. Not, get drunk and act crazy." Rell's three compadre's give him a "you're kidding me" stare and start laughing. They re-ignite their boisterous chant. "More drinks! More drinks!"

All of the tables have candles burning. Rell's chanting buddies began to pound the table. Someone starts the generator. The lights come back on.

His friends stop and look at each other. Their smiles grow by an inch. Pounding harder, they cheer louder, "More drinks! More drinks! More drinks!"

Rell is really embarrassed by his friends' actions. He tugs on his tie as he clears his throat. He doesn't do it to prepare himself for a speech; it's just a nervous reaction he's had since becoming a banker. He's been grabbing his tie since the day he became a loan manager. It started at his first meeting before the board and since then he's been trying to end the bad habit.

He holds his hand up and gestures for his buddies to stop. "C'mon, guys," he says.

They ignore his pleas and continue their incessant pounding. Laughing as he shakes his head, Rell looks around the table to his friends who are misbehaving. There's Phillip, the architect of the bunch. He considers himself to be the undercover player of the crew. He even considers himself to be Denzel Washington's twin. Then, there's Reyquan with his low cut and wavy hair. He's a construction worker. Rell pauses as he thinks, "Yeah, Reyquan must be drunk because his light-complexioned-ass is starting to look oily. On top of that, he can't even speak any Spanish! To make it worse, he's the only one of the bunch who can't keep a job. He's of Peru-bean descent but has never even tried to speak any language other than English."

Reyquan's the college gangster of the bunch. He's on his sixth year of medical school, but he's not sure whether he wants to pursue his rapping career or become a doctor.

The waitress brings more drinks over. Rell cuts in, "Hold up fellas, c'mon, don't let Carlos drink too much – you know how he is when he gets drunk."

Carlos waves his arm over the table like it's a giant crystal ball and slurs as he speaks, "Toooooo laaaaayte, my man." His head wobbles as he giggles, "I'm alllllready toorrree up."

The waitress sets the drinks on the table while the three friends give their fourth amigo a quizzical glance.

As he reaches for another drink, Rell folds his arms and says, "See, I told you. And y'all know this dude likes to fight."

Their drunk friend twists his lips. "Yep! I suuurrre doooo!"

All three look back and forth to one another and speak in unison, "Ah, damn!"

Reyquan turns to his intoxicated pal. "C'mon Carlos, don't do that stuff tonight."

Carlos gives a devilish grin and begins to gleefully nod his head like a child who's been asked if he wants cookies from the jar. "I want to fight," he replies matter-of-factly.

Rell checks his grey Armani suit to make sure everything is in place before he removes his coat. The last time Carlos got drunk and started a fight, he'd ripped Rell's Sean John suit that Rell's wife had purchased for their anniversary.

Carlos goes acapella and starts to pound on the table by himself, "I want to fight! I want to fight!"

His friends hold their heads low, and they attempt to quiet him.

Phillip is sitting next to Carlos and tries his best to calm their friend. Phillip knows if he doesn't calm him down, and Carlos gets in any kind of altercation, that he and his friends will attempt to stop it; however, each and every time, someone has always gotten hurt in some form or fashion.

Reyquan is also clearly drunk. He begins to cry. "Man, we're friends – why do we have to fight all the time?"

Phillip and Rell look at one another. The two, start laughing because this is how it always happens. Carlos wants to fight, and Reyquan wants brotherly love.

Reyquan continues, "Man, we've been friends since we were all five years old!" He points at each of them, one at a time. "You, you, and you. Maaaaan, we don't need to fight. Come on, Carlos, let's not fight tonight."

Reyquan is sitting on the other side of Carlos. He hugs his friend and cries on his shoulder. Phillip and Rell just stare at the two drunkards and shake their heads.

"Ohhhh-kaaaay!" Carlos cries, "I won't fight anybody tooooo-night!" And then he yells to the people inside the lounge, "I'm not going to fight tonight, because one of my brothers doesn't want me to hurt anyone!"

In return, everyone shakes their heads and waves him off. Some even throw their middle fingers up at him and call him a pussy.

The storm must have passed over, because the sound of the thunder seems to be farther away. It's still raining cats and dogs though. You can tell because you can hear the strong waves of the wind, and heavy droplets of water, clashing against the outer shell of the building.

People are still running in from outside. There are two young ladies who look to be in their twenties, a husband and wife, and some older lone white guy in a tan trench coat who rush inside the door. He looks like a pissed husband that's trying to sneak a quick drink in. Two more men walk in; they all head straight for the bar.

All is quiet at the four friends' table. Reyquan and Carlos are still hugging each other, while crying; Phillip is resting his chin in the palm of his hands as he stares at the odd "Couple of the Year"; and, Rell is just sitting back, laughing to himself. First, he's happy that he's the designated driver tonight; and second, because he can't wait to clown the two cry-babies for not being able to hold their liquor.

Someone bumps into the back of Phillip's chair. He's a little tipsy, but he's not drunk. He turns back to see who the rude person is that doesn't know how to say excuse me. His face knots up as he turns to inspect the obvious drunk.

Before he can face the waitress, she pats his shoulder. "I am so sorry. Please forgive me."

Phillip and Rell both sit up at attention. The first thing they both notice is her curvy figure. Her waist line is small. Her thighs are thick and she has a strut of a supermodel.

She interrupts their gazes by clearing her throat. "Excuse me, I'm up here," pointing to her face.

After looking at her sexy tight smile, her smooth mahogany skin, and her deep beautiful brown eyes, Rell speaks first. "Oh, he doesn't mind a little bump."

Phillip jumps back into action. "You damn right, I don't mind – but I can only forgive you if you sit and have a drink with me - oh, and my friends."

She licks her lips. "Well, I'm working right now, but I was really interested in meeting your friend, " she points to Rell, "right there."

Immediately, Rell is speechless. He already has enough relationship problems at home with his wife, Sheila. For over a year, they have been talking about getting a divorce. The only thing keeping them together is their two children, lil Tyra and Trevon. His jaw drops.

Phillip cuts in, "Honey, why don't you come back over when you have your break – from what I can see, it would make him happy."

She smiles and blows a soft kiss to Rell before slowly walking away. She even glimpses back a couple times before she makes it to the next table.

Rell closes his mouth. "C'mon, Phil, why did you do that? You already know that I have enough problems." He slides his chair back to get up, and he bumps into someone behind him. He glances back, "Excuse me, I apologize for that." He turns back to Phillip. "Now, I have to go over there and tell her I'm not really interested. You really like making me look like a fool or something?"

Phillip doesn't respond; he only smiles as he sips his drink. Rell shakes his head as he backs away from the table. He bumps into the white guy with the tan trench on.

"Sir, I apologize again. I didn't..."

The trench coat grabs him by his neck from behind. He slings him all over the place, knocking over Rell's friends' table and a couple others.

Reyquan and Carlos look up. They jump to their feet, along with Phillip. Rell is gasping for air. The man in the trench is extremely strong.

Rell is a refined man, but he knows how to take care of himself. He came up the hard way. Like some hard-working people, he was raised in the ghetto; and like many, he set his goals very high. That being the case, he and his friends got into many fights while growing up in the rough streets. At young ages, they swore to always protect one another.

Struggling to free himself, Rell almost throws up at the smell of his attacker's breath. The Man in the Trench Coat reeks with cheap alcohol. Rell is slowly squeezing his hand under the aggressor's arm. His attacker is sticking to him like glue, but if he can just get his arm free.

A circle is created by the on-lookers. Some of them are holding Rell's friends at bay.

"Just another inch," Rell thinks as he forces his fingers deeper under the man's forearm.

Suddenly, Rell is slung to the floor, and The Man in the Trench Coat stands over him. His voice is rough, like an old, wet power saw: "You fucking nigger! You want some of me? Don't worry; I'm going to kill you, you fucking nigger!" He slowly turns to Rell's friends. "I might just kill all of you! I hate all of your kind – you filthy bastards!"

Rell jumps to his feet. He's ready now – face to face, but a bouncer jumps in his way. Two people grab him from behind. If he could only get to him, Rell know's he can take his attacker.

Rell fights and pulls to free himself. The more he breaks free, the more hands grab him. As he struggles, he watches the greying man who just attacked him walk away.

The Man in the Trench Coat is about six feet tall. He looks to be in his forties. He looks like he used to play football in his youth. His hair is salt and peppered colored, and his eyes are a solid black with a hint of death in them.

An insane expression appears across Rell's face as thoughts flash through his mind: "Damn, maybe I was wrong for bumping into him twice. He probably thought that I was trying to pick a fight with him. I'm a grown man – I shouldn't be acting like this. I guess, I have to suck this up..."

He then looks to his friend's that are fighting to free him from the crowd. Rell quickly relaxes his muscles. He calms himself. "I'm cool!" he yells. He raises his arms to the air, "It's over! He's gone and I'm not trying to fight! It's my fault – I'm sorry for interrupting all of your nights!"

As soon as his words drop from his tongue, the lounge becomes quiet. The storm is the only thing that can be heard in the background with the distant thumping and pounding of thunder and the constant crashing and rattling of the wind and heavy rain. Everyone is motionless. It seems like they are waiting for a movie producer to say "cut!" or something.

Finally, the hands are falling away from Rell's upper torso. As they drop like flies, Rell begins to fix his clothes as he and Phillip inspect each other's eyes. Rell, gives the" nah, it isn't worth it" look. He then searches for Reyquan. He finds him standing in his ready for battle stance – he's not crying anymore, either. All three of the friends turn to Carlos' position. He's not there.

Searching the entire place, they spot him staggering toward the bar. They turn back to each other and shake their heads. Rell displays a silly smile as he thinks to himself about the whole mix up.

The crowd begins to dissipate. They are all going back to their tables. Rell and Phillip grab for their seats to sit back down but before they can even twist their chairs to their direction, Reyquan, waves his hand wildly in front of their faces. He's pointing to the entrance with his other arm.

The friends then whirl toward the entrance. It's Carlos. He's staggering out behind The Man in the Trench Coat. They all take off behind him.

Outside, they quickly spot their friend at the end of the block, turning right at the corner. Running behind him, they stop at the corner. They're already breathing hard.

"Where did he go?" Phillip asks.

Pointing to the left, Rell answers, "Look! There he is ... right there!"

Carlos had crossed the street, and he's cutting in between two buildings. His friends are back in hot pursuit.

They end up in an alley. Reyquan points, "There he goes!"

Phillip and Rell ask at the same time, "Where?"

"He's down there at the end of the alley!"

The three tired friends charge his direction. While in pursuit of their buddy, thoughts begin to flow through Rell's brain. He's hoping that his longtime friend is in good condition and that he can find him, before something bad happens to him. He knows that the guy who attacked him had to be crazy, because nobody in their right mind is going to jump on three nice-sized black guys' plus a big Peru-bean black guy. Not by himself. No way. The Man in the Trench Coat is crazy.

They can see him now. The gap is closing. He's only a few yards in front of them. Suddenly, a figure jumps out from behind the bushes. He lands on Carlos. Carlos is too drunk, and he falls over like a sack of potatoes.

It's The Man in the Trench Coat, but he took it off. It looks like he has a knife in his hand. He's stabbing at Carlos. Carlos is waving his arms all over the place. He's trying to get away from the crazy man.

The rain is pounding the concrete. It seems like the clouds are trying to flood the world. It's dark and the rain is thick. It's difficult to even see in front of you, but Rell can see that his friend is in dire need of his help – and he needs it quick.

A burst of energy floods into Rell's veins. His heartbeat quickens as the speed of his feet elevates. He runs with all of his might to get to his long-time compadre.

Before he even gets within five feet of Carlos, he leaps with determination and tackles the knife-clincher. He breaks Carlos free, but now he's stuck with the unwanted problem. The two roll over for a while until Rell breaks free and stands up. The Trench Coat Man jumps to his feet, too.

Rell holds his hand up to his friends, "You guy's stay out of this! This shit's between me and him!" After his friends stop, he focuses on the old drunk: "Listen, for many years I've dreamed of beating the shit out of a racist bastard, but I was wrong for bumping into you – I'm sorry, we don't have to do anything stupid!"

The drunk only laughs at him, "You niggers! You're so stupid. You're dead." He lunges at Rell with the knife. "I'm going to kill you!"

As he lunges again, Rell knocks the knife away from his hands.

At first, Rell is happy that he finally gets to whip a racist person's behind; however, his dream is immediately tarnished at the sight of the pistol handle that the The Man in Trench Coat just placed his fingers around. Without a thought of hesitation, Rell retackles the drunk.

Phillip, Reyquan, and Carlos all look ___ with amazement; no matter how intoxicated or what frame of mind, they all know that Rell knows how to fight with his hands. He's been considered to be one of the best boxers from the old neighborhood, so why did he tackle him after he dropped the knife?

As the two wrestle on the pavement, a gun suddenly goes off. Then, it goes off a second time. The two fight to their feet. They're still locked into each other's grip. A car pulls up from out of nowhere. It drives up to within an inch of the brawlers and blows its horn.

The gun drops to the ground. Rell and his opponent slowly step back. The Man in the Trench Coat places a hand on the hood of the car and falls down to the pavement.

As his opponent drops, Rell can finally see something that he didn't notice at first: The guy is wearing a police badge. His brain switches to slow motion mode. From the man's lifeless face, to his stiff body... and then to the dead fear in his eyes, Rell's mind overloads with the visual before him. It hits him ___ The Man in the Trench Coat is a cop.

Rell's brain shuts down. The only thing he can hear is the distant sound of the thunder: Boom! Boom! Boom! He also hears glass falling around him. He thinks, "What did I do? God, please help me."

In a flash, he's being jumped on. Someone is jumping on his back. He can hear a voice. Who is it? Wait, he recognizes the voice. It's Phillip.

Phillip shakes him, "Rell, come on – they're shooting!"

Rell's thoughts come back. The car, someone is shooting through the windshield. He can feel his feet again. He and his friends are running. He doesn't know why, but tears are coming from his eyes. He thinks again, "Oh God, what have I done?"

Chapter Two

The police frequencies are going crazy, all over the radio it's heard: "Officer down! Officer down!" Radios are cutting in and out, "Detective O'Brien is down...". The air wave goes quiet for a moment; silence by itself describes the grief.

A cry comes on the wave, "This is Detective Brewkowski! Please tell the ambulance to move faster; we need them here, now!"

The dispatcher comes on, "Are there any suspects?"

"Yes, three to four black males!" Brewkowski peers down to inspect his dying partner. "I couldn't really see what they were wearing; it looked like the shooter was wearing grey or black slacks and a white button down." He releases the button to make sure the dispatcher got it all, then he presses it again. "The suspects ran east toward Crandum Street."

Around the city, it seems like all police sirens came on at the same time. It's still raining outside, and blue flashes of police lights are reflecting from every building in town as they speed to the aid of the fellow officer.

The four friends are running for their lives. They're running so fast that it seems like the ground no longer exist. They can hear the sirens as they reach their cars.

Phillip sounds off, "Yes, now we go to the police."

Rell refuses, "No, let's get out of here."

Becoming confused, Phillip asks, "Why not?"

"Listen to me! Let's just get out of here. We can all meet at your house. . . .and I'll tell you what you want to know when we get there."

Phillip, Reyquan, and Carlos all analyze Rell who's - shaking from head to toe. He's extremely pale, and he's standing stiff as a board.

As the sirens draw closer, he cuts in. "C'mon guys, I promise I will explain why at your place." Pointing to Phillip, he repeats himself. "C'mon, I promise."

They decided against their better judgment to go with their longtime friend. Whatever the case, Rell needed some help, because he was in a very bad condition. The four determined that it would be better for Rell not to drive because he doesn't look too good, and since Reyquan came with Carlos, he decided to drive for his friend. Rell is riding with Phillip, because Rell really needs to be around someone who is a good listener and someone with some legal skills.

Back at the crime scene, the site is gruesome to a policeman's eye. A highly decorated detective lies dead on the ground. He had to die in a back alley. He landed on his face, in an alley that no one in their right mind would be caught in, and died alone. He had to die at a job that very few people even have the courage to do. He had to die, while his loved-ones were at home, waiting for him to walk through that front door.

The hardest job for any officer is to deliver the message to a loving family. No one wants to tell a wife or a husband, a child or a parent that they will never see someone they love anymore. Most officers would rather be the demised than to have to be the messenger.

The radio air wave is buzzing; suddenly, it comes in: "He's gone. Detective O'Brien is gone. We lost him. ."

The radio flat lines.

Minutes later, Chief O'Conner arrives on the scene. He leaps from his car and rushes over to O'Brien's body. The area is being lined with the yellow tape. The chief is clearly upset. His face is red with pain and frustration.

After viewing the body for a few seconds, the chief yells at the top of his lungs: "I want the murderer found, and I want him or them all found before sunrise!"

Chief O'Connor is usually a very humble and warm-hearted man. His parents where descendants of Ireland. He was raised the Irish way. He's a tall James Bond looking guy. His hair is dyed a dark umber. He's wearing his jogging suit.

He just got back from his trip to Ireland. He spent his annual time at Killarey Lakes fishing. The last thing he wished for was to come back to something like this.

A car screeches as it comes to a stop. Its occupant leaves the door open as he runs over to the chief. It's Captain Smith. He's still wearing his robe and his slippers, as well as his firearm.

As he draws closer to the chief, he yells: "I want you guys to set up a one-mile perimeter and canvass everything from two blocks back to this spot!"

Before the captain makes it to the chief, the chief spreads his arms wide and says, "Alright, I don't want anyone beyond the yellow tape but the forensics team." As he walks away from the murdered cop, he signals for the captain to rendezvous with him by his car. He yells, "This is one of ours; I don't want anyone to mess this up!"

Captain Smith is one of those cops that joined the force to stop the inner-city racism between the old white cops and the poor people of color. He grew up in Harlem when there weren't many black cops. It was a time when, even in your own neighborhood, your rights were very limited as a person of color.

As a young child, Captain Smith made his decision to become an officer of the law after he witnessed two cops beat his father. Supposedly, they thought he stole a purse from an old white lady.

Later, Smith joined the Marines. After he served his term, he became a Jersey City policeman.

Captain Smith's large frame moves with ease. He may be close to retirement, but he's still fit as a teenager. He begins to explain his poor dress code to the chief.

The chief cuts him off. "I know – you didn't have time to get dressed, because you wanted to get here ASAP. But, I didn't call you over here for that; I called you because I want you to know that this is personal."

He steps closer to the chief. "Excuse me, sir?"

"I'm saying this is a very important case," reiterates the chief.

"Sir, I understand this – O'Brien, is one of ours."

"No Clerance, he's not just one of ours. I practically raised him. I knew his father very well. His father was my mentor. His father trained me before he died in the line of duty. In fact, his father's last request to me was to take care of his boy." The chief points to O'Brien's body. "I want whoever killed him – in cold blood — in jail before dawn."

Phillip and Rell make it back to Phillip's place. Rell's body language hasn't changed; he's still a nervous wreck. Then again, he seems to have worsened since the last time anyone checked on him. He's extremely paranoid. He looks like his body's temperature has dropped by forty degrees, and his eyes are blood red with stress and worry.

Phillip's wife and four-year-old son become frightful at the sight of their visitor. Phillip's wife quickly sends their child to another room. Just like a toddler, he playfully wobbles away.

Phillip asks his wife to give him and his friend some time alone. He then grabs a chair for Rell. After Rell sits, Phillip grabs a chair for himself and sits right across from Rell.

"Alright Rell, what was it that you wanted to talk about?" Phillip asks.

Rell doesn't respond; he only stares into an empty space.

"C'mon, man, tell me so that we can make our next move."

Rell mumbles, "He was a...".

Phillip is becoming agitated and spouts back at him. "What? He was a what?"

"A cop." A tear escapes from Rell's eye as he thinks about his words.

"Whoa. Are you sure?" Phillip becomes nervous by just the thought of what his friend is saying. He searches around his kitchen like he has something hidden in it. "I mean... are you sure he was a cop? And, how do you know he was a cop?" Phillip asks.

Continuing to speak with a dead mumble, Rell tells him what he saw. "I saw his badge when he fell to the ground. His badge was hanging out of his shirt pocket."

Phillip has an epiphany. "Wait— I know it's bad, but you only defended yourself. He attacked you, and you have me, Carlos, and Reyquan as your witnesses." Feeling more relaxed, Phillip jumps to his feet. "Another thing, where was his back-up? Why was he walking around or even hanging in an old alley, jumping on people's backs? That doesn't sound like a cop to me. Man, don't forget, you did have a couple drinks." Phillip's mind is spinning out of control with questions.

Phillip seems to have convinced himself. He parades around the room. "Man, do you know how many jobs require people to wear badges?" Walking back to Rell, Phillip continues talking. "Hey man, get your mind right. We can get through this."

Phillip's son calls for him. He doesn't hear his son calling out the first three times. When he finally hears him, he calls his wife and asks her to check on him.

A little color returns to Rell's face. "Yeah, maybe you're right; but still, I killed a man tonight." The glare of misery lingers. "And, the police are probably searching for the murderer as we speak."

Sighing, Phillip sits back down. "How do you know that you...," he asks, checking his rear to make sure his wife is not in the room and then turns around and whispers, "...killed someone? The man might still be alive at a hospital or something."

Giving a faint smile, Rell sits up. He says, "Hey, you may be right. He probably is alive. I mean, the gun went off, in between us, and it didn't hit me – it could have missed his vital areas, as well."

Phillip's son charges into the kitchen. "Daddy!"

Phillip calls for his wife. "Wanda, could you please get him for me?"

Ignoring his father's serious conversation, he tugs on his daddy's pants leg. "Daddy, Uncle Rell's car is on TV."

Rell and Phillip make eye contact as they both head for the living room. The word "panic" lands right in the beam of their sight. The duo stop in their tracks at the first glance of the TV screen.

The child was correct— it's Rell's car. A brand-new Silver Lexus LS 500 has been in a serious accident. The Lexus ran head-on into a light pole. The news anchor reports that the car had to have been speeding in order for it to have been wrapped around the concrete beam.

It doesn't take long for Rell to recognize his car, because he notices his chromed factory rims that he had put on the car himself, and his A-plus student bumper sticker that he only placed on the back windshield - a few days ago. His license plate is hanging to the ground, but he can clearly see his plate number.

The reporter comes back on. She states that both occupants were dead on arrival. Then, she further states that the impact was so powerful that the faces are unrecognizable, and that the police believe the accident was alcohol-related.

Phillip's wife is sitting on the couch with her hands covering her mouth. His son, oblivious to the situation, is running in circles chanting. "I told you. I told you. I told you."

A tear drops from Rell's eye as he grabs his son. "Come on, son, I need you to go to your room for your bedtime."

"Ahhhhh, Daddy – do I have to?" he asks.

"Yes, you do... Daddy needs you to give us adults some time to talk."

He gives his father a curious inspection. "Daddy, you and Mama always say that, but all I ever hear is 'hmmm', 'ahhhhh', and...".

His mother cuts him off. "Sergio, go to your room – now!"

The child bows his head and pouts his face as he exits the room.

The three turn to each other as Wanda speaks. "Oh my goodness, what are we going to do? We have to get down there to make sure this is not a mistake." She was expecting a response, but no one says anything. "Are you guys listening to me?" Wanda asks.

Her husband and Rell want to listen, but an emergency report just flashed on the television. The reporter comes in at a grisly murder scene. It's a dark alley. The two friends look at each other.

They zoom in. The reporter standing in the rain announces that there is a city-wide manhunt for a killer. She then turns to a detective, but he is unable to speak. He's heart broken. His partner is the deceased. It's Detective Marten Brewkowski. The reporter turns back around and explains that an officer has been murdered in cold blood.

Phillip's wife is talking, but the two fail to hear anything that she says.

Finally, Detective Brewkowski comes to the camera. His eyes are as still as death. The reporter speaks to him; however, he doesn't even respond to her. Brewkowski already has a message in mind.

He grabs the microphone from her hand and speaks coldly and calmly. "If the murderer is listening, I want to give you the opportunity to turn yourself in before it's too late." He wipes his eyes. "If you're scared of being hurt, don't worry. I will personally make sure that you are brought in safely – just turn yourself in." Brewkowski finishes, staring dead into the lens.

He returns the mic to the reporter and walks away.

Rell's legs are weak. His head is light. He feels oozy in his gut. He forgets that Wanda is in the room. He faces his longtime friend. "I'm a dead man."

Chapter Three

Ryan Brewkowski walks back into the crowd of his peers and superiors. They're stunned by his actions on television with the reporter. They all watch him as he heads back to his car and sits back in the car seat with a blank face of grief.

Detective Brewkowski drops his face into his palms. The grief is overwhelming. The two had been partners for 15 years. The two-man team had spent more time together at work than they each had spent at home with their own families. They each knew the other's deepest secrets, greatest achievements, favorite foods, and even little things like how to prepare one another's coffee. The two had a bond that was like a professional marriage.

The raining finally stopped. The entire alley is lit up with spot lights, patrol car lights, flash lights and, of course, the weak alley lights. The yellow tape has been stretched into a large square shape, sectioning off the center road of the alley. A team of homicide detectives is searching the grounds outside of the caution tape while the forensic team has the inside perimeter under a magnifying glass.

Chief O'Connor places a hand on Brewkowski's shoulder. "Son, I know this is hard for you, but you already know the only way we can get those bastards who did this is by getting a statement as quick as possible."

Brewkowski nods his head and begins to speak. "We were here on a B & E case. We discovered that our suspect might be in this area." All of the Officers are completely quiet as Brewkowski continues, "O'Brien wanted to go in under cover and draw the suspect out into the open."

Chief O'Connor interrupts. "What's his name? Who is he?"

Shaking his head, Brewkowski answers. "We never knew his name. Our informant only told us that the possible thief might be between these few blocks. He said that he was planning on robbing something in this area tonight."

Chief O'Connor steps back as Captain Smith steps forward and kneels down before him. "Listen, I understand that this is difficult," he pats Brewkowski's knee, "Just tell us exactly what happen in this alley." The captain knows that this is a very sensitive issue, and he doesn't, want to use the word dead or anything in relation to it; so, he only emphasizes it with his eyes. "For now, we need only to know what happened tonight in this alley. – we need a better description so that we can find the guy or guys responsible."

Clearing his throat, Brewkowski tries again. "Marten – I mean. . . O'Brien, was trying to fish out the burglar who's been hitting a lot of places in the area." Taking a deep breath, he continues, "O'Brien went into a local lounge; he wanted to be perceived as a local with a bad drinking habit." He begins to breathe deeply. "And that's when I lost him..."

Captain Smith snaps, "You lost him?"

"Yeah, I didn't see him again until I seen him fighting with the shooter in this alley." Brewkowski is hyperventilating before their eyes. "I didn't even know it was him at first. It was raining too hard. I heard two to three rounds discharge. That's when I sped over." He drops his head. "I was too late... O'Brien was hit... I watched him drop," Brewkowski says and points to the scene, "Right over there." Sobbing and stomping his foot, he confesses: "I could have saved him."

Chief O'Connor interjects, that's enough, son, what did these guys look like and who's your C.I.?"

"Like I said, the shooter and his friends were black. I couldn't see exactly what they were wearing, because it was raining so hard out here, but the shooter was wearing a white button-down collared shirt with dark-colored slacks. His hair was low cut, and it looked like his face was a cleaned shave; but, because it was raining, I'm not really sure." Brewkowski tries to remember as much as possible.

Chief O'Connor draws a pad from his pocket. "Alright son, who's the informant? I want to send someone over to question him."

He shakes his head. "The C.I?" The crowd around him closes in as he shakes his head some more. "I don't know the C.I."

Chapter Four

Crowds of reporters have surrounded the front of the podium. They're waiting for the public briefing on the murdered officer. Everyone is standing shoulder to shoulder with their cameramen and the other reporters. Thin electricity wires and various thick cables are stretching at the crowd's feet, connecting a plethora of reporting equipment to their vans with the satellite dishes.

All of the reporters are watching the entrance to the precinct, anticipating the arrival of the mayor and his small entourage. Some of them are quiet, and others are yapping about what to expect.

Suddenly, shushes are heard as the mayor leads the way to the podium. He's followed by the commissioner, the chief, and five other people with pens and pads in their hands. Two are women, and three are men. They all sit in the chairs that line the temporary stage.

Another woman walks out the door. She's the public relations officer. Stepping to the microphone, she clears her throat as she sets a piece of paper on the stand next to her folder.

The reporters are silent. They're all holding their recording devices toward the speaker.

Clearing her throat again, the public relations woman checks the mic before she utters anything. "Hello, everyone. I wish I could say good morning, but today will not be good until this case is closed," she begins. A reporter holds his hand up to ask a question. She stops him. "There will be no questions today. This is only a briefing." The reporters all look at one another. She continues, "Last night, at approximately 8:30 p.m., an officer of the law was murdered..." She allows her words just a second to stick to her listeners' thoughts before she keeps going. "Detective Marten O'Brien was a twenty-year veteran. He died at the scene of the crime. So far, we have very few leads in our state-wide manhunt... which is why we're asking the public to call the number, listed at the bottom of your TV screen, if you have information that may be of some use."

As the public relations brief is being given across town, Captain Smith has called an emergency meeting. Most of the officers at the meeting are in on their scheduled shift, but there are many who've decided to work double shifts until they get the murdering perp off of the streets.

The tactical briefing room is similar to a college class room. It has five rows of six school desks sat parallel to each other. The captain is standing next to a platform. On each and every desk lies a folder and a pen, just in case someone needs to take a few notes. Some of the officers are leaning against the wall in the back.

The captain's face doesn't look too good; it's obvious that he didn't sleep too well last night. He knows that for every minute the suspect has on the street, the colder the case can get. It's been over twelve hours already; and, as far as they're concerned, the scumbag might be in Idaho – there's no time for mistakes.

"Morning", Captain Smith says. As he walks around the stand to get closer to his staff, he continues. "On each of your desk, you will find a photo that we got from the cruiser last night." Tightening his fist, he explains that "the picture is not too good, but it's all we have until we get a better lead." He speaks louder. "I want each one of you to get out there today and get us a better lead for our Marten O'Brien."

Policemen around the room are nodding their heads in agreement. Their morale is high. Their determination is apparent, some more than the others. A group of Irish officers sit in the back of the room, huddled in a circle. They're not even paying attention to the captain; they have their own plans and tactics for finding the murderer. Without warning, they storm to the exit.

The captain pauses from his briefing. "Hold up, where are you guys going?" The pack continues their march for the door. They are moving so fast that the captain can't think of their names quick enough. He calls the first three of them: "O'Dougle, Colgan, and McRiley. . . You all stop right there!" They all stop as the captain storms over and says, "What is the meaning of this?"

Sergeant McRiley turns to the captain. Before he gets within five feet of him, he spouts, "Captain, you don't understand how serious this is... He's one of ours."

"How serious this is? One of yours?" The captain mimics, shaking his head. "Look, I don't need you guys running around out here tearing up this city." He moves to the door and blocks the men from exiting. "Listen, Marten is and will always be an honorable man of the law. He is a part of every person in this room, and even on our police force – you men will not turn this into some kind of wild rodeo for the Irish. We are all lawmen, and we will follow the law - I will have you all thrown off the force before dinner if _____."
He points his index finger to the desks. "Now, I want you all to have a seat, so that we can finish

this briefing; then, we can all go out there and get this perp!"

The group reluctantly sit back at their original places. The captain returns to the front of the class room. This time the entire atmosphere is very different. Everyone in the room can see the devastation in the Irish officers' faces, and all in attendance want to make sure that they do their part in catching the bastard that has done this.

Everyone opens their folders. The picture is basically a blur in the night. It's plain to see that it was raining too hard on the night of the murder to make out any distinguishing characteristics. On the photo, you can clearly see that it was a black man who was fighting Detective O'Brien, but you can barely see any good details. Like Detective Brewkowski said, "He's wearing a dark-colored pair of slacks with a white shirt and dark-colored tie."

As the meeting ends, the team of Irish officers are the first to run from the room. The captain attempts to call them back, but he changes his mind – there's no time to waste on each other; they need to find this killer.

Chapter Five

It's Monday morning. Phillip is getting dressed. His wife is already up and preparing their son for school. Rell is still stressed and waiting on the couch.

Rell and Phillip have decided to try and wait until after their friends' funerals before Rell even attempts to turn himself in. He feels, in his heart, that he won't be able to get bond – not for a murdered cop. Rell will remain at the apartment while Phillip goes around and takes care of everything for their deceased friends.

Walking into the room, Phillip inspects his friend sitting on the sofa. "Hey, I have all of your insurance information for your car. I'm going to call Sheila when I leave, and I'll also be checking on Reyquan's and Carlos' families."

Rell hasn't been able to sleep the entire weekend. His head is throbbing, his body is aching, and he still doesn't have a clue as to what to do. He only nods to his friend's remarks and points to the television.

On the screen, the news anchor is replaying the cold and distant message from Detective Ryan Brewkowski. Rell is immediately trapped in the nets of his eyes.

"Do you see him?" Rell mumbles. "He is hurting like me. He must know something." Rell looks up to his friend. "I bet you he knows that his partner was drunk."

Phillip nods his head. "But, don't forget what I already told you – we're talking about a cop – not some drug dealer, a cop. These cops are going to try to beat your brains out before you make it to the station. Phillip places his hand on Rell's shoulder. "Give me some time to get you an attorney." He cuts a smile in. "Plus, don't forget that I already told my wife that you're only here because you and Sheila are going through some problems."

Rell responds without moving his head from the TV. "Yeah, but don't forget that everybody knows that Sheila and I have been having problems for a very long time now. So, what difference does it makes if she finds out that I am now a cop killer..."

Phillip throws his palms to the air. "Shhhh, man be quiet." Phillip steps back to make sure that his wife is still in the other room with their son. He whispers, "Look Rell, I know that you are going through some major stuff, but don't forget that you're the only brother that I have left. I don't want to lose you, too, at least not like this. Man, I know that you're innocent. So, don't start acting like it's just you— by yourself– against the world." Phillip lets out a sigh.

Rell turns the channel. Once again Detective Brewkowski is on television, but this time he appears to be drained of all anger. His grief is displayed all over his face. He begs for the killer to turn himself in – and if the killer feels that he is in fear of being hurt by anyone, he can call Brewkowski's personal line for a safe trip into the station. Detective Brewkowski's number flashes across the bottom of the screen.

After checking out the number, Rell twists around to his pal. "Phillip, please just do me this favor. Call this guy and let him know that the guy who he thinks murdered his partner in cold blood is innocent. Let him know that it was all a mistake. I only fought in self-defense. I only wanted to live..."

Shaking his head, Phillip says, "Are you crazy?"

"Nah man, I just want him to know that it was an accident."

Wanda interrupts the two as she announces her and her son's farewell.

Phillip's son yells, "Bye, Daddy! I love you!"

Phillip turns away from his depressed partner. "Okay. I love you, too, son!"

A faint smile grows on Rell's face as he hears the child calling out to his father. Once Rell hears the door clapping against its frame, he stops Phillip from talking. "Listen, I know it may sound crazy, but I just need someone to at least speak on my behalf. I'm only asking that you call his number and let him know that I..." He pauses and recants his statement. "I mean... call him and let him know that the accused shooter is not on the run, but only preparing for a legal battle, because I am – I mean, he is an innocent man."

"Hold on for one second," Phillip says, holding up his index finger. I want you to think for a second: Who in hell do you think was shooting at us? I want you to really think about it." Phillip backpedals and leans against the wall. "I know we don't know who it was, but don't you think it was his partner?"

"No, I don't think it was his partner because I didn't hear anyone saying 'stop, police.'" Rell stands and says, "I didn't even hear him talk about it on TV."

"Man, are you crazy? You really think that they would mention that on TV?" In frustration, Phillip twists his face and throws his arms up in submission. "You know what? I don't even feel like arguing with you about this... I'll do it, but I'll call from a pre-paid cell phone. Alright?"

Rell sighs with joy. "Thanks, man."

Phillip grabs his coat, but before he leaves, the two plan their next rendezvous to be about three hours later. Rell is too nervous to sleep, so he sits and browses through the televisions channels. He doesn't want to use his phone, because he doesn't want to argue with his wife Sheila. He knows she's probably calling him like crazy to curse him out right now. This is why he turned his phone off the first night he didn't return home.

A couple hours have passed. Rell's still sitting on the couch clicking the remote. He's amazed at how many channels his friend has on the television. He's always known that cable companies provide customers with many channels, but he never expected the selection to be so full of pay-per-view stations.

He grumbles with frustration. "These damn pay-per-views..."

Rell finally finds an old Godzilla movie. He leaves it there, because he doesn't want to see anything that might remind him of his current problems.

He gasps as he stops his breath. He thinks he's heard someone lightly tap on the door. Turning the TV down, he listens for it again. "Oh shit," he thinks, "someone's tapping on the door."

He wonders, "Who could it be? Who would be tapping on Phillip's front door? Is Wanda cheating on him? Is someone doing that, because they want to make sure no one's here, before they break in?" His eyes open wide. "Oh shit, someone's going to break in – what do I do? I can't call the police." He searches for a weapon.

Running into the kitchen, he eases a drawer open. Damn, it's only spoons and forks. Moving slowly, he slides another one open. Jackpot – it's the knives. He retrieves a huge butcher knife.

He heads for the front door in an attempt to scare the crooks. To his amazement, the thieves are already opening the door. It's opening very slowly.

Rell tiptoes to the coat rack behind the door. He holds the knife high in the air. He's already killed one man. He doesn't want to kill another person, but what if the person wants to attack him? He begins to tremble with uneasiness and grips his weapon tighter. Holding his arm up to stop the door from hitting him, he opens his mouth to say something— but nothing comes out.

The door stops before it even gets close to him. He's sweating with uneasiness and fright.

He's still trying to speak, but still no words are coming out.

Suddenly, the door begins to slowly close. He becomes saucer-eyed. It seems like the door is moving a thousand times slower in its reverse mode.

"Wait a minute", he thinks, "what are those?" He squints his eyes. "They're fingers..." Squinting harder, he discerns they're a woman's fingertips. The door closes and he looks up.

Sheila screams at the top of her lungs.

He screams, too.

Sheila grabs for the door to run for her life, but she realizes it's only her husband holding the knife.

Rell gets a better view of his woman and tucks the weapon behind his back. "Hold up. What are you doing here?"

Holding her chest as she breathes heavy, her mouth is dropping open with surprise and shock. "What am I doing here?" Getting her thoughts together, she continues, "I came here to look for you, because I knew something had to be wrong for you not to come home. Don't forget, me and Wanda are girlfriends." Her husband's eyes stretch wide. "Oh yes, Wanda gave me keys to the place."

Sheila smiles as the words leap from her lips: "That's a woman's power, dear."

He can't help but to smile back. Going over his wife's beautiful frame always brings back some of their sweetest memories. Rell inspects her rectangular shaped glasses that give her a look of sophistication; her silky, long black hair that she usually keeps in a ponytail (but today she's allowing it to lay across her back); and the hard nipples of her perky breasts.

To his amazement, she's not wearing her medical coat that he usually sees her in at work, but he quickly remembers that she probably left it on the coat rack at her office. His wife is a radiologist, and this has always turned him on, because even as a child – C'mon, who doesn't play Ms. Nurse and bad boy patient?

She steps forward as he admires how well his wife looks. She's always been a great dresser. She's wearing a beige cashmere D & G turtle-neck sweater and a black skirt that's really fitting her thick, tone thighs extremely well. The honey-cinnamon hue of her skin definitely highlights her attire. He steps away – yep, her little pigeon-toed feet look so cute in her tan Roberto Cavalli knee-high boots.

His mind begins to drift to the past – when the two first met. It was at Payne College in Augusta, Ga. He was going to Payne, and she was at the Medical College of Georgia. It was Wanda who introduced them one night. Wanda didn't want to go out with Phillip by herself, so she set up a blind date for his friend. It was love at first site for a long time, until things started to go downhill over the past year or two – people never really remember when the problems began – they're just happy when everything is over.

There was a time when the couple could do nothing but think of making love and having children – but that all ended after their second child. In the beginning, the pair would wake up singing love songs to one another, and they would walk and hold hands everywhere they went. They would kiss before every meal, before they went to sleep, and even before the sun came up. . . and then one night, things completely changed.

Sheila seemed like she never wanted to leave work; when she finally did come home from work, she refused to sleep in the same bed as Rell. In the early days of their relationship, just a simple touch of her body would spark a passionate fire between the two. But now if he touches her, she screams, "not now". Sometimes when he gets home, he catches her in a mirror, staring at his back like she wants to put a knife in it. It's extremely obvious– the love has been gone for some time now.

His brief smile quickly fades. "Sheila, I don't have time to argue with you. There's just too much happening right now."

She takes the knife from his hand and places it on an end table by the couch. "Rell, honey," she says as she stares into his lonely eyes. "I know, baby. Wanda told me about how bad you've been feeling. I also saw the car on the television the other night." Placing her warm hands on his arms, she says, "The police have been by the house." He tenses up, and she quickly consoles him. "Don't worry, baby, I told them that you were away for the weekend."

He smiles. "Thanks, love." He flinches because he hasn't called her that nickname in a long time.

"What did you call me?", she asks.

He chuckles. "C'mon, you know what I just called you."

"I know, dear – I just love seeing that lost smile of yours." She pinches his cheeks and kisses his lips. "That's a thanks, for calling me your love again."

He moves from her; his grief is back. "Sheila, what am I going to do? Reyquan and Carlos are both dead."

She steps closer. "You're going to do what you've always been able to do. You're going to pull through this." Sliding her arms around his waist....

"Do you remember when your grandfather passed?" she asks him.

He looks away, but he nods his head.

"Rell," she waits until he turns back to her, "you pulled through, didn't you?"

He smiles once again. She has this effect on him. All of this time, through the good and the bad, she still has that power over his heart – it's hers to do whatever she wants with it – he can't stop loving her even if he tried.

Reaching around her slender waist, he reaches down like he used to do, and squeezes her perfectly soft derriere. Without thinking, his fingertips gently travel past her butt cheeks and stop between her thighs. He becomes aroused by the heat from her hot abyss of passion. His eyes are closing; he's high with the urge to make love to his woman.

"Oh, shit!" he exclaims and draws his fingers away. "I apologize." Purring like a cat, Sheila moans in his ear. "Oooooh honey, you can touch her; she's still yours." Squeezing him tighter, she says, "I've been waiting for you to touch me like that for a long time – please don't stop now."

In a flash, all of the bad nights disappear. It's like Rell has turned into some type of wild animal. He's gripping her back with one hand as he sucks on her neck. He uses his other hand to find that soft, sweet, wet spot again...

She's moaning louder. She's sucking on his ear lobe as she raises one leg. "Damn!" she exclaims. The length of her skirt stops her leg from going all the way up.

She reaches down, pulls her skirt up, and raises her leg. "C'mon, baby, give me some." Whispering into his ear, she says, "You already felt how much I want it."

His fingers rub the outside of her panties.

"Oh God!" Humping his palm, she pleads, "Rell, please fuck me."

Her dirty language drives his mind wild. He growls like a hungry lion and rips her panties from her hot body. He grabs for her dress next, but she stops him.

"Don't forget, I need to wear something out of here."

He squats down and throws one of her legs over his shoulder. He shoves his face deep into her steamy, hot pussy. As soon as the juices hit his face, he licks and sucks her clitoris like it's his last meal.

It feels so good to her; she stumbles as she works to unzip her skirt. "Oooh, yes baby." Grabbing the back of his head and pulling it in with her free hand, she tells him exactly what she wants him to do. "Eat this pussy. Eat it baby."

Rolling her neck back, she yells out. "Oh God, eat all of me!"

Rell begins to rotate his face around like a blood hound that's searching through some bushes. She is groaning out of control. He stretches her leg higher. He wants to dive deeper into her abyss. She tastes so good to him. He misses this taste. He's hungry for her love. She pulls harder on his head as she gyrates her lower body over his mouth.

Pulling his face back for a second, he admires how the desired area is so cleanly shaved. He licks his lips in delight as he thinks: Damn, my baby's pussy, is still thick and phat."

Sheila pulls him up. "C'mon, baby, you know I want to have some fun, too." Dropping to her knees, she looks up to him with an innocent pout, and teases him. "Are you going to stop me?"

Her husband quickly shakes his head and drops his pants in a blink of an eye. Grabbing his johnson, she gazes at its hard form while throwing her hair back. First, she kisses the head of it – Rell thrusts his hips forward, bumping her lips lightly.

She shakes her finger side to side to her husband. "Uh-uh, he's mine now – and I know how to treat him. So you stay out."

She slides her lips around his manhood slowly. Rell's back arches over. She knows exactly what she's doing. This is her weapon against him. She almost swallows him whole.

His lower jaw drops open. It's been so long since he's felt his wife's tongue against his stiff, throbbing organ.

She grips him firmly, and begins stroking him as she sucks him. His hands find their way to the back of her head. He humps as he pulls her closer. She doesn't stop. She loves the feeling of his need for her.

Backing away, as she continues to stroke, she asks: "Did you miss me, baby?"

Nodding like a five-year-old, he replies, "Yes love – I've missed you dearly."

She smiles and begins to suck the side of his penis. She doesn't stop stroking; she's just sucking from one side to the other and licking his lower abdomen.

His head is rolling in circles. "" Oh, yes, love. Oh, yes."

She then holds his stiff rod up and begins to suck his testicles. His arms have fallen from her head, so she stops. She knows all too well that this is a sign that her man is about to cum, and she doesn't want that – not yet, anyway.

Rell looks down. "What's wrong? Why did you stop?"

His wife doesn't respond. She stands up and the two kiss passionately. He reaches down and grabs her rear-end again and, of course, he eases his finger to her love spot. She slides his johnson in between her legs, allowing her the right to feel him pulsating against the walls of her soaking wet insides.

After a minute, she steps away. She stares him down, taking her time to remove her brand-new sweater. Dropping it to the floor, she gives a devilish grin. Her nipples are erect and ready. Her firm breasts are begging to be touched.

He reaches out, but she steps back.

She smiles as she plays with her skirt. The remains of her shredded panties fall to the floor. It only takes a second for the skirt to land on top of them.

She is standing with nothing but her knee-high boots on. Her body is flawless. Placing her hands on her waist, she spreads her legs apart—like she's a super hero or something.

Rell grabs for her again.

She moves toward the couch, evading him. She walks to the center of the living room. Her man watches her from the rear; he is astonished by the fact that he can see the gap between her thighs.

Her folds are thick, and her juices are as sweet as homemade pecan pie. He watches her body as she moves across the room; her sweet spot peeking out from between her toned thighs like a cinnamon-colored rosebud.

She stops in the middle of the floor and resumes her wonder woman stance. "C'mere baby."

Rell removes the remainder of his clothes as he rushes over. The couple meet with an urgent desire to please. Rell gently runs his hand through her hair as his tongue greedily enters her mouth.

Sheila reaches down and grabs his cock. She slides the tip of him between the lips of her moist center, thrusting her hips back and forth.

She stops kissing him and drops to the couch. "C'mere baby, I want you now." Seductively, she spreads her legs wide. "What honey, you don't like my boots?"

He laughs at the playful banter. "Oh, you got jokes, huh?" He places his hands on her hips and pulls her to the edge of the couch. He eases his manhood inside her, smiling as he watches her sweet, pink slits part to consume him. He thinks to himself, "It's been so long." She pulls him toward her. He begins that familiar rhythm: in and out, in and out.

Scratching her lover's back, Sheila begs, "Oh baby, give it to me. Yes, yes, oh give it to me." Pulling harder, she demands more. "Fuck me, Rell – fuck me."

No words leave his mouth; he only arches his back more and thrusts harder and harder, deeper and deeper, rotating his waist in a circular motion.

Not wanting them to part for long, Rell secures his arms around her and moves her body down the length of the couch. After he lays her back down, he grabs her by the waist and reenters the wet place that makes all his fears disappear—at least for right now.

Looking down at his bride, he thinks about how he misses making love to his little Georgia peach. Her body is so immaculate to him. He smiles, looking into her eyes– so much woman in a hundred and twenty-pound frame.

Her eyes are beginning to roll back, and a smirk develops on his face. He knows she's about to have a toe-curling orgasm. He knows what time it is – he keeps hitting that spot; he knows exactly how to make her feel like she's floating on air.

Someone knocks on the door. Sheila gives him a "forget-that-door" stare. She's cumming – and cares nothing about who may be at the door.

The knock turns into a banging on the door.

Rell finds himself cumming, too.

BOOM! The front door is knocked in. "Police! Get down!"

Rell wakes up on the couch. He's sweating like a four-hundred-pound man in a sauna. Wiping his face, he checks his watch. It's been well over the three hours that he and his pal agreed to; it's going on five o'clock.

He laughs to himself because no matter how angry he is at Sheila; he can't get her out of his mind. He still misses her gentle touch, but the pain returns–the pain of knowing in his heart that they may never regain what has been lost.

Checking his watch again – yep, it's after five p.m.- Rell quickly reflects on the backup plan that he and Phillip decided on prior to Phillip leaving. Feeling his pocket, he finds the keys to a small apartment upstairs.

Phillip uses the tiny space upstairs for his additional office work. He always has plenty of blueprints to look over and or design, and the small work area allows him somewhere to keep the prints away from his four-year-old son. Also, Phillip and his wife like to creep up there when they need some adult time.

The two decided that if Wanda returns home for her lunch break or for any other reason, Rell would go up to the upstairs apartment and wait until Phillip comes back.

Rell opens the door to the apartment. To his surprise, it's nice. It's a typical bachelor's pad. The place has a midsize couch, a nice dining set, and even a single size bed.

Rell shakes his head. "I see why Phillip took so long to tell me about this place."

Walking over to the window, he closes the blinds and peeps out. He's becoming more confused by the second and wonders: "Where is this guy? What's taking him so long? Why didn't he at least call?"

Looking around the place, he thinks, "Well, I'm not going anywhere until I hear from him." Jumping to his feet, he checks the refrigerator and sighs with relief at the sight of essentials. "Yeah, I'm not going anywhere until I hear from my man."

Chapter Six

It's been over a week since Detective Martin O'Brien's murder. The entire city is on lockdown. The news channels have been constantly tracking this story.   Even Chief O'Connor has been repeatedly seen on television, advertising a reward for any information that could lead to the murderer's arrest.

The forensic team has a specialized group of digital photo specialists working to clean up the video from the night of the homicide. An FBI agent was even sent in to oversee the meticulous task.

Today is a very special day for the Jersey City police force. Today is the day that they lay their fellow brethren to rest. Today is Detective Marten O'Brien and his family's day. Today is the burial day.

A convoy of motorcycle patrol men lead the hearse into the cemetery. The hearse is followed by a limo and a huge fleet of patrol cars from New York, Hoboken, and Jersey City.   There are no sirens, but all of their lights are flashing.   The length of the civilian's line is even longer. There seems to be almost a thousand guests.

The weather is nice. The sun is out with a cool spring breeze. Only a few clouds linger in the sky. In fact, the clouds resemble beautiful mountains, floating in a perfectly deep blue ocean, miles above the earth.

Most of the guests have found their seats that have been set up across the lovely dark green lawn. The bag-pipe musicians are positioned to the left of the visitors. The rifle guard is to the right of the guests. Marten O'Brien's wife and close family members are sitting in the front – right in front of the empty hole.

A group of men are standing at attention at the rear of the hearse. They're in full police regalia. It's the Honor Guard. The on-lookers are respectfully quiet as they remove the body from the vehicle. Once the men all have their hand in its correct position, the leader whispers his commands and directs the group to the burial site.

Everyone admires the casket as it draws closer. It's a pearly creamish color with gold trimmings around its borders. Its frame is a bit wider than the average casket, because its occupant isn't a small guy. His family and friends also wanted him to have the best, all the way to the end.

The casket is sat in its place. The leader of the honor guard nods to the priest, giving him his cue to speak.

The priest clears his throat before initiating the eulogy. He opens his bible.

As the preacher begins to quote some verses from Psalms, two men are standing at a distance from the funeral. Usually at any other funeral, these two guys would be sitting with the guests, but this is different – these two men are with the IAD (Internal Affairs Department).

Joseph Brown and his partner Tom Riley aren't here for an investigation; they're only here to pay their respects to an officer of the law. The only problem is that they are still on duty.

Joseph Brown, also known as Big Joe amongst the IAD, is the quiet type. He's up tight today, because he's never liked seeing any officer of law get laid to rest before their time. He tugs on the neck of his sweater. It feels like it's choking him.

Tom spits to the ground with disgust. He knows how his longtime partner feels. "You alright, Joe?"

Chewing on his straw, the big guy doesn't say anything.

He doesn't bother to repeat his question. He already knows the quieter his partner is, the angrier his partner is.

Tom places a hand on his partner's shoulder. "Hey big guy, you wanna leave?"

Big Joe shakes his head no.

Let the truth be told: Tom Riley, is the hot-headed one. He's the epitome of a fiery Irish. He's the type of guy you'd gladly give five feet of breathing room after a few drinks, because you know he's always looking for a good fight. Luckily for everyone, he stopped drinking almost ten years ago – then again, that didn't have any effect on his hair-trigger temper.

Combing his fingers threw his rusty red hair, he stops and thinks: "This could've been my funeral. Me and Marty grew up together. We went to the same schools and grew up in the same neighborhood."

Tom's temperature begins to rise. He unbuttons his brown blazer as he mumbles. "We're going to get the bastard who did this."

Big Joe doesn't say anything, He only cuts an eye at his partner. He's been living between New York and Jersey long enough to know that the Irish are a very loyal group of people. This is why he chose Tom as a partner, he loves loyalty.

The priest finishes his sermon and summons the City Commissioner to the podium.

Tom watches the commissioner unravel his notes as he prepares to speak. Big Joe taps Tom and nods his head in the direction of O'Brien's wife.

It doesn't take long for him to notice why his partner pointed her out. She's sitting up front, ignoring the entire eulogy. Her eyes are everywhere like she's doing anything she can to keep from focusing on the funeral.

She curls her lips as soon as the commissioner says something. The two partners glimpse at one another. She continues to frown at the commissioner's comments; she even laughs at a couple of them. Some of the guests who are sitting close by even take notice; they frown their faces with disgust.

Tom turns to big Joe and gives him a "maybe-she's-drunk" look. They both shrug their shoulders with confusion. Though neither is saying anything, red lights are flashing in their minds. What's wrong with her? Is she drunk or something? Is this how she handles her stress? Did she discover a mistress or an ill-gotten child?

The two take a closer look: She doesn't seem to be a woman in mourning. There is no running mascara – she hasn't shed one tear. She's not even wearing a black dress or a veil. She's wearing an expensive gray dress that's really fitting her svelte body, and entirely inappropriate for a funeral...let alone that of her own husband.

The preacher comes back up and calls on any family members who may want to speak. She doesn't even flinch.

The IAD partners shake their heads. Not because she didn't get up to speak- it's common for some wives not to be able to speak at their husband's funeral- but because of the way she was rolling her eyes as if she was loathing the mere thought of having to speak.

The partners wonder what's wrong with her. Why would she act like this?

Debbie O'Brien is a very attractive, petite blond. She's half Irish and half German decent. Her frame matches her long hair- the curves are all in their right places.

From the beginning, Marten's family complained about him marrying a woman who was so many years younger than him. They met five years ago, when he was forty-one and she was only twenty-nine. She was still into partying, and he was just an older man who was happy to have a younger woman interested in him. After six months of dating, the two married and proved everyone wrong – she was happy to become a house wife.

Family and friends are lining up to view the body. She doesn't move. Her face becomes indifferent. There is no sign of joy or grief, or anything really. She's just sitting there with her legs crossed like a respectful lady, resting her hands on her knees.

Tom and Joe are still watching her crazy expressions and movements, or the lack thereof. A few people are blocking the duo's view from time to time as they pass Mrs. O'Brien to view the body, but their sight is only obstructed for a few seconds at a time. Suddenly, a man approaches her. He walked up to the receiving line with the other guests. It looked like he was trying to see Marten's remains, but he jumped from the line as soon as he made it to the front row.

Stopping and kneeling before her, he pulls a manila envelope from the inside of his coat. He hands it to Debbie and whispers something in her ear. She's nodding to whatever he's saying. It only lasts a few seconds, and the strange man is gone. She's left clutching the envelope.

The priest comes back with his final words.

She can't wait. She slowly opens the envelope and picks through its contents.

After closing the service, the preacher signals the commissioner. The commissioner then orders the honor guard to fold the flag. As soon as this happens, the bugler blows the sound of taps through his brass horn.

Debbie doesn't move her eyes from the inside of the envelope. Something catches her attention. She cuffs her mouth with her hand.

Tom doesn't tap, but instead hits his partner. "Are you looking at this?"

The rifle guard lets off the first round of their gun salute; it catches most of the guests by surprise and causes them to jump.

Even Debbie jumps, but tears are beginning to fall from her eye sockets.

More shots are fired, however, this doesn't deter the IAD partners' attention from the strange acting widow.

With every boom of gun fire she jumps, but she doesn't stop reviewing the items inside of the manila container. Her palm is glued to her lips – whatever it is, she's shocked to see it. Tears have fallen beyond her cheeks to her dress.

As the last rounds are fired, the honor guard passes the commissioner the folded flag from the casket. He turns around and proceeds to give it to the wife of the fallen officer.

She's holding a photo, just above the brim of the envelope. She looks up just as the commissioner approaches her. Quickly, she drops the photo back into its container. Without giving a second glimpse, she jumps from her seat and walks away from the funeral.

The commissioner is left standing there with the flag. All of the guests and him are shocked by her abrupt exit. His face is full of bewilderment.

The IAD partners remain quiet like the guests, and I look on as Ryan Brewkowski rushes to the aid of his deceased partner's wife... He reaches her before she gets to her car. Grabbing her arm, he pulls her close and whispers into her ear.

She struggles violently to get free. He draws her closer to himself and hugs her before speaking softly to her.

The onlookers give a deep sigh of relief, because he seems to have everything back under control.

Suddenly, she screams something unintelligible to him. Everyone is quietly trying to cipher her last words, but before anyone can do so, she breaks free of Brewkowski's hold and jumps in her car.

Brewkowski runs to the driver's side door. She ignores his pleads and hits the gas. He's left standing there in a cloud of dust.

Chapter Seven

Sheila awakens to a bright and beautiful morning. It's about seventy something degrees outside. She hops out of bed and covers her mouth as she yawns. She leaves her two children, Trevon and Tyra, laying across the bed as she tip-toes into the restroom to brush her teeth.

At the mirror, her eyes become watery again. She can't get the memory out of her head. The thought of having to view and identify the bodies from the accident. She's rejoiced that it wasn't her husband,

To make it worse, the police made her answer what seemed to be a thousand questions about her husband while she stood over the zipped-up body bags containing the bodies of Reyquan and Carlos. She's never felt more depressed in her life. "What happened to my husband, and where is he?", she thought.

Across town, the apartment building is surrounded. A four-block radius is closed off. A patrol car is parked at every corner, deterring all traffic away to a safe area. A few pedestrians are complaining about not being allowed into their community. Everyone is inquiring as to why they're being halted, but the police are tight-lipped.

If a tenant looks out of the windows of their apartment building, they wouldn't know that it is surrounded. It's peaceful outside. The sky is clear and sunny. Cars are parked in their usual places. The electric company workers are working on a light pole. There's a couple sitting in their car having a serious debate; it seems like they're about to end the relationship.

A cable company van pulls up. Its driver jumps out with a cheerful grin. He walks to the entrance of the building with wearing a million-dollar smile.

There are four SWAT teams already positioned in the building. They are double checking their gear. Each is wearing a solid Kevlar helmet with either a pair of goggles or a sturdy pair of glasses. They're also wearing ballistic vests with a twelve by twelve-inch plate at the center of the chest. The knee pads, the groin protector, and even the elbow pads that some are wearing are all made of Kevlar, too.

Most of the SWAT are carrying HK MP5's, M-16A2 Commando's along with a variety of hand guns. Their weapons of choice range from Glock-17 9mm's to Smith & Wesson's 357. A couple of them are holding the Remington 870 mini shotgun with cut down barrels and pistol grip handles.

Before coming to the location, the SWAT had a meeting discussing the makeup of the entire building. It was decided that the team will be listed alphabetically A through D. A-team is to hit the primary entry from the north front door. B-team is to target the rear, and C and D are to monitor the side apartments for any signs of escape.

Rell is sitting on the couch, chewing what's left of a bag of peanuts. He's making the best of it, because he knows there's not much food left. There's only a little junk food and a few snacks remaining in the fridge and, even though he's at the point of destroying his muscular physique, he knows he'll have to eat the junk food sooner or later.

His cell phone begins to chirp. He only turned it on to call Phillip. He doesn't press send because it's his wife, Sheila. Finally, his voice box kicks in and he picks up the call.

The cable man makes it to the floor. He easily finds the apartment. There it is down the hall. His feet move with ease as he approaches the door.

Rell can hear someone outside in the hallway. He catches his breath as he slowly presses down the SEND button. He doesn't drop his eyes from the door. The cool touch of the glass and metal rests on his ear lobe.

It's too late. Her screams can be heard before he gets a chance to hang up. "Wheeeeeeere. . . have. . . you. . . been?" she hysterically wails.

Rell coughs. "Huh?"

"Don't you huh, me", she spats. "Where have you been, Rell?"

He remains tongue tied. His eyes are still glued to the door. He wants to hear where the footsteps are going.

Sheila continues, "I've been worried about you. The police have been to our house about fifteen times."

The word police brings him back. "POLICE?"

"Yes, they've been asking about the accident that Reyquan and Carlos had in your car."

Suddenly, someone knocks on the door. His jaw drops to the floor. In his mind, the words OH SHIT are flashing faster and faster.

His wife continues her diatribe. "I can't believe that you would leave me and the children

behind   at   a   time   like   this."
He tenses his fingers around his phone as he whispers. "Shhh, be quiet for a second."

The phone goes silent for a moment. "Uh-uh, who are you telling to be quiet? The children have been asking about you for over a week. You haven't called – not once- to check on us... Don't you ever tell me to be quiet when you have a family that's concerned about you."

He holds the phone away from his ear as he watches the door. There's another knock. This time it's heavier. Rell isn't going near the door, because he doesn't want the person to see his shadow approaching the door through the peep-hole. His breath quickens.

The cable guy repeatedly knocks on the door, but no one answers. Reaching under his clip board, he clasps the handle of his firearm and glimpses to the SWAT team at his right.

After the SWAT leader nods back, he then issues his ultimatum. "This is the Jersey City police department! You may come out with your hands up, or we're coming in to get you! You must surrender in order for us to help you!"

Still, no response...

The SWAT team leader gives him the signal to back away from the door. The team then eases closer to the side of the door. They're all crouched down, waiting for the go signal.

The A-team consists of four men. Each is carrying the M-16A2 Commando. This fully automatic machine gun was specifically designed for urban warfare. Its frame is feather weight. The rifle butt is adjustable and its muzzle is shortened to ensure that the shooter is able to easily move around during battle. This weapon will chop a person down before they even realize they've been shot.

Within seconds, the signal can be heard. It's the sound of breaking glass and a flash bang landing on the apartment floor.

A flash bang is about the size of a soda can. It's a grenade used to throw off one's equilibrium by giving an explosive bright flare and an amazingly loud bang with a hundred and seventy-five decibel crack. It usually leaves its victims looking clumsy and stupid all at once.

The grenade goes off. The SWAT team has a man use a door ram to take down the door. The back is entered at the same time. Team A enters the front and follows the borders of the wall. Each cop following behind the next, each weapon aimed in a different direction.

As the two teams make their way through the apartment, they shout "clear" to one another every time a room has been checked and deemed safe.

The teams have checked the entire place, except for one final room. It's the last room at the end of the hallway. They all approach with a slow but steady pace. The leader of B-team kicks the bedroom door open.

There's a man sitting on the bed. He's wearing a bath towel around his waist. His hands are resting on the edge of the bed. You can plainly see that he's trying to keep himself stable. His eyes are distant and glassy, which is what happens when a flash bang lands in your house. It leaves you stupefied.

The teams grab him and cuff him. They don't dress him; they take him the exact way they found him.

Back at Phillip's place, Rell remains on the phone with his wife as he watches the door. He doesn't even try to stop her from fussing. He simply sets the phone on the couch and stares at the direction of the knocking sound.

Finally, the person at the door walks away. Rell's heart slows as the shadow's feet move from the entrance.

After a few seconds, he eases the phone back to his ear. He clearly hears his wife huffing and puffing on the other end. He thinks for a second how she's always had that sexy way of getting her way whenever she pouted, whether it be in his presence or on a phone. She'll always have him, when she wants him.

He speaks with his softest voice. "C'mon Sheila, you know I'm not trying to abandon you or our children... I love all of you – you're my family."

Before he finishes his words, Rell can hear his son asking if that is his father on the phone.

She sighs and asks her son to go into another room. The receiver comes back to her ear. "Okay. Since you looove us so much, why is it that you have two dead friends – that died in your car – and I haven't heard from you in a whole damn week?"

The word DEAD lands right in the center of Rell's aching heart. His chest becomes hollow every time he thinks of his best friends.

He loses the bass in his voice. "Sheila, you don't have be so cold. C'mon, you've known the two of them for a long time, too, or are you just that wicked now?"

She didn't mean to talk the way she did. She's only angry because she hasn't heard from the father of her children in over a week. It has nothing to do with Carlos and Reyquan, directly, but it has everything to do with his responsibility as a father and a husband – which is why she's working so hard to emphasize the seriousness of the problem at hand. However, to a certain degree, she's out of line. A lot of her words are coming from the major problems within their marriage.

In the beginning, there was never such a thing as anger or animosity between the two. That's when the pair lived like a couple out of a romance novel. A few years down the line things changed for the worse, and now it's difficult for her to remember what it's like to speak softly to her husband.

Sheila clearly hears and understands the grief that's coming from her husband's sluggish, hurting heart. She knows that she may be angry with him, but she's not a wicked lady.

A faint tear seeps down her cheek. "Rell, I seen their bodies." Weeping in between her words, she goes on. "I could barely recognize them... They burned in the car fire."

"The car was on fire?" he gasps.

"Yes, it caught fire after the accident. They said it was your gas tank." She hears his phone drop. " RRRREEEEELLLLLLLL!!!! Are you okay?" She's crying.   "Rell baby, pick the phone up. Where are you?"

A minute passes, he picks up the phone. His voice is weak like a man who's on his deathbed. "Hello."

She pleads, "Where are you? I'll come to you."

"I can't let you come. I'm in a lot of trouble right now."

"Rell, I'm your wife. Honey, please tell me what's wrong."

He whispers even lower. "I can't – especially on this phone."

"You can't tell me where you are? Or you can't tell me what's wrong?" Sheila asks.

He begins to mumble something, but she cuts him off with an exclamation of shock. "Oh my God!"

Rell's voice comes back. "Huh, what is it? What's wrong?"

Her lips are quivering. Her hands are shaking. She throws her hand over her mouth as her jaw drops.

Again, RELL asks, "Sheila, what is it? What's happening?"

She screams at the kids. "Get out of this room! Go play outside!" She waits until they leave the room. Rell is literally sweating bullets.

Drawing the receiver closer to her lips, she whispers like someone is standing next to her, trying to eavesdrop on the conversation. "Rell, you're on television. Your picture is on T.V . . . You're wanted for killing a police man."

His heart begins to race again. "Sheila, are you sure it's me?"

"They don't have your name, but they have a digitally enhanced photo of you from the night of the murder."

"But... how do you know it's me?"

"I know it's you, because I can clearly see the suit that I bought you... Rell, you can see your face clear as day – it's you..." The phone goes silent. She continues to call out, "Rell! Rell!"

He mumbles some words.

She retorts, "I can't hear you."

Rell repeats, "I said I'm at Phillip's place."

Chapter Eight

Joseph Brown exits the elevator. He greets his fellow coworkers as he heads toward his desk, which is situated right beside his partner's desk.

There's no office for the two of them. In fact, only a few people who work within the internal affairs department have an office – and they are all much higher in rank.

The Internal Affairs Department is set up like most. It consumes the whole floor of the building. All of the big shots have offices located along the outer walls of the building, each with its own window, and the rest of the IAD employees reside in a bunch of cubicles throughout the center of the room.

Big Joe makes it to his cubicle. "Whoa!" He's startled by his partner. "What are you doing here?"

Tom grins and shakes his head. "I couldn't..."

"Hold up – and you have a clean shave. What in the hell?" teases Big Joe.

"Okay big guy. That's enough. I've already heard it all from the rest of the department."

Joe sets his stuff on his desk. "Okay – then tell me before I start thinking that you've lost your mind or that your wife has finally gotten the sense to leave your crazy ass."

"Ouch. That hurts – even coming from you, big fella." Tom throws his feet up on his desk as he leans back in his chair. "I'll have you know that me and my ex-wife – that already had enough sense to leave me last year – went to church together this past Sunday."

Big Joe shakes his head. "No... please don't tell me you're back with her. She's the one that almost made you relapse." Sitting on top of his desk, Joe keeps going. "Yeah, you remember. . . I'm the one who almost had to draw a gun on you just to keep you from taking a drink?" He leans in closer to his Irish buddy and whispers. "Do you remember how you stopped that guy who was drinking while driving – just so you could take his beer for yourself?"

Tom laughs. "Oh, I did. Didn't I? That was funny, too."

Jumping to his feet, Big Joe is done with the conversation. "Man, I don't have time for this stuff, again."

Dropping his own feet to the floor, Tom tries to clarify. "Hold up, big fella. We're not getting back together. I just needed someone to be with me when I went to church, and I couldn't reach you."

Holding his palms to the air, Joe is even more confused. "Hold up. What did you wanna go to church for?" he asks Tom.

Tom lowers his voice. "I needed to go, because I really needed to clear my head. I've been doing a lot of thinking about Marten O'Brien. I mean, you seen how his wife was acting at his funeral – and she didn't even wait until the end of it. I couldn't sleep right after I seen that act of hers. I mean – it's still bothering me."

Joe sits back down. "I know what you mean. Something doesn't seem right." He stares at Tom's fresh cup of coffee. "I mean – did you see how Ryan Brewkowski, followed her to her car? I know she had family there, too, but he was the only one who chased her to the car." Big Joe reaches for his partner's coffee. "I mean...".

Tom snatches his cup from the desk. "No way, bro. Get your own cup this morning. I really need mine today."

The big guy sighs. "Man, you owe me a cup from the other day when you stole my cup from my desk."

Not putting up a fight, Tom gives in and starts laughing. "Alright, I'll get you a cup but not this one, big guy. Taking a sip, Tom leans back in his chair. "Nah, I'm kidding. I'll get you one in a minute, but right now I want to hear what you think about this stunt of Marten's wife."

Big Joe pulls a pen from his pocket and begins to scribble something on his pad. "Well, let's look at it. What was she reading in that envelope?" Joe asks aloud. Tom tries to say something, but Joe holds his hand up and continues. "What did she see or hear to make her leave so abruptly? I mean, think about it – she didn't even arrive in the limo with the rest of the family."

Setting his cup on his desk, Tom attempts to talk again. "Yeah, wait a second... She drove her own car. What type of widow would come to a funeral in her own car?" Big Joe reaches for the cup again, and Tom moves it farther away to the edge of his desk. "And did you see how he whispered something into her ear?"

The two begin to shake their index fingers at one another. The fiery Irish jumps to his feet as he points at the big guy. They both initiate a grin, followed by a light laugh.

They speak in harmony. "They're having an affair."

The big guy sits down. "But, what does this have to do with Marten's death?"

Tom ponders the question for a second. "Well – I don't know. Maybe Brewkowski could've saved his partner but didn't do anything because he wanted Marten's wife for himself."

"Hey, that's a good point. However, we can't prove it. . ." Big Joe meets his partner's gaze. "Yet!"

Someone runs out of a nearby office. "Hey! They have a suspect in custody!"

The two men become saucer-eyed as they look at each other. They both race from their cubicle and march to their captain's office. They're not running, but they're racing each other while walking at their top speed. The rest of their co-workers are migrating toward the announcer of the good news. The pair stop right at their supervisor's door, each waiting for the other to knock on the door. Suddenly, the door is opened before them. It's their captain.

He looks from one to the other, "Can I help you fellas?"

The partners look to each other first before turning back to their boss. They speak together. "Sir, we need to talk to Detective O'Brien's murder suspect."

He growls, "You two, come in and have a seat."

The IAD pair shrug their shoulders as they look to each other, before they step in the office and take a seat.

The captain's office is plain, but nicely designed. A large brown wooden desk sits at the center of the room. On the desk, the captain's computer sits on the left and there's a stack of papers on the other end. He's sitting in a huge black Barcelona chair. His plaques and awards hang on every wall in the room. By the door behind the two men, a cabinet is displaying photos of the captain's family. The office seems to be very comfortable.

After staring at the two for a few minutes, he asks, "Alright, what do you two want to talk to the suspect about?"

The two talk for about ten minutes. Telling him everything they had witnessed at the funeral, from the apathy of the widow to the romantic moment at her car. The captain remains silent the entire time. However, at the mention of the mysterious envelope, his eyes widen.

Once they finish, the captain doesn't say a word. He only twists his monitor around and points at the screen. He presses the play button.

On the screen is an autopsy report. Tom asks, "Sir, who's that for?"

"That's Marten's report," the captain says, pointing to the far edge of the screen. "You see the level of alcohol in his blood?" At the sight of it, the two partners are stunned. The captain continues, "Yeah, he smelled like a busted-up liquor store when his body was picked up from the ground." He looks to the both of them to make sure that all of his words are settling into their thoughts. "Detective Ryan Brewkowski also reeked with alcohol at the scene of the crime. Our informer says Brewkowski smelled like he tried to use mouth wash to hide it, but it was still very obvious."

The partners lean in closer to their captain giving him that "so-where-does-that-leave-us" look.

The captain searches the faces of his two detectives as he speaks. "I want you two to find out exactly what happened out there that night, because I agree with you – something doesn't add up. If you two have your gut feelings, and the rest of us have these crazy test results – I definitely want you two to investigate this matter."

They smile with appreciation. The two stand as Big Joe reaches out to shake the captain's hand. "Sir, we'll go and interrogate the perp right now."

The captain gives a saddened truth. "Wait, don't worry about that. We've already heard that he has a pretty strong alibi. I think they were only trying to appease the public." All three look to one another with agreement. "Yeah, the department had to lock someone up. It's starting to take too long to rid the streets of a cop killer."

Big Joe speaks with content. "And that's what's so strange. What's taking so long? We have a file on every, or just about every, thug out on the streets, and we haven't found this one yet."

Tom rubs his knee. "I hope it wasn't a mob hit, because I will personally take them all down."

The captain cuts in. "Nah, it was too sloppy to be a mafia hit. If that was the case, we'd already have heard it on the streets by now. You know they have more snitches now than ever before."

Tom looks up. "Don't forget – we have many mafia groups between here and Boston. What if it wasn't the Italians we're talking about?"

The captain turns the monitor back around to himself and begins to press buttons. He finishes typing, turns it back around to the pair, and points.

Tapping the screen, the captain shows them. "You see that? On the screen is the picture of the murderer looking right into the camera of the patrol car. The face is plain and clear. Look at him." He presses another button and the picture shows the suspect standing over Marten's slumped body. His index finger taps the screen again. "You see him?" His eyes grill the two detectives. "If you two don't find out what's going on – that's a dead man standing. We have to find him before the police force kills him." He zooms the photo in and repeats himself. "He's a dead man standing!"

Chapter Nine

Rell sits on the window, peeping from behind the blinds, watching down below. He's constantly reflecting on his last phone call with Sheila. She wasn't at home. She was at one of her girlfriend's places. This is why she never saw Phillip. He must have gone by the house after she left.

But, where is Phillip now? Rell's mind wanders. "Why hasn't he come back to check on me? Is he downstairs with his wife? Is he trying to negotiate a deal for me? He's always had that hustler in him." Rell smiles at his last thought and then, he thinks harder. "It's been over a week. I haven't seen him come through the front entrance. Maybe, he returned through the back entrance or the basement. Maybe, he was followed and he's too scared to come up. Then again, I have seen his number on my missed calls list. Yeah, I just need to wait a little longer." He looks to the land line. "He told me not to use that – so, yeah, I'll just wait. He's not going to let me down."

There she goes; it's Sheila. His eyes open wide. She's moving from side to side as she breezes past other pedestrians on the side walk. She did like he asked her to. She parked four blocks away and walked here.

Her stride is strong, graceful, and seductive all in one. You can see in her walk that she is a beautiful and confident woman. She grips her purse tightly as she marches like she's singly stampeding towards battle against an army of hungry lions.

A faint glow of happiness appears on his face as he watches his lady charging to his rescue. He's seen her come to his aid before, but it's been so long he's forgotten what it was like.

It happened one night in Augusta Georgia when the two decided to take a stroll down the river walk that bordered Augusta's city line and the South Carolina's state line. The lovely couple were gazing at the beautiful scenery of the city's own version of the Roman Theater and its many lights that trail the river.

Suddenly, Rell jumped on top of one of the benches and stumbled to the ground. It was at that moment that he saw all of the love and compassion that she had for him. He had only sprained his ankle, but she didn't care. She leaned him on her shoulder and struggled to carry her man back to the car. Even after weeks of her care, and his ankle fully healed, he refused to lose the love that she shown to him. That was the moment when he knew that he was going to make her his wife.

She cuts past a businessman talking to his friend. They both stop talking as they stare Sheila down. Rell's face tenses as he grills the men down with his eyes. He never did like any man looking at her like she was just a piece of meat. She's much more than that – she is and will always be his queen.

Rell gives a deep sigh as she enters the building. Many wonderful thoughts pop in and out of his mind as he ponders all the ways he plans to caress and hold her. Wait. . . he sees strange movements below. It's the two men that were ogling his wife. They're following her. His breathing quickens. The two men move swiftly – in her pursuit.

There's more movement. Three more men are rushing across the street. They're all wearing trenches. Rell realizes these men are police, not the casual businessmen he initially thought them to be. He can tell, because he works around them all the time at his bank.

To assure himself, he rationalizes the situation. For what other reason would there be five white men, cleanly cut and trimmed hair, waiting outside of a building to follow a woman to a supposed cop-killer?

Rell grabs for his phone. It seems like it refuses to allow his fingers the chance to grip it. He pulls the excess junk from his pocket – used napkins, Phillip's apartment keys, and a couple pieces of lint. He grunts as he finally grasps the phone.

While watching the men below, his throat constricts as he sees one of the men's assault rifle peeking from under the trench. He becomes faint at the thought of being killed. He calls Sheila's phone. It rings repeatedly. She's not answering.

He glances back out the window. All of the men are inside. He's really becoming nervous. He continues to call her over and over. Every time her voicemail answers, he hangs up and tries again. His heartbeat is racing.

He looks at the door. He doesn't even realize that he's talking aloud. "I need to get out of here." He runs over to it and checks the peep-hole. He whispers "it's clear" and opens it. Looking into the hallway like a schizophrenic, he continues talking to himself. "I can't believe she would set me up like this." Rell sticks his neck out farther into the hallway. "That greedy bitch wants the damn reward." Suddenly, the hurt hits him. "I loved her. We have children together – and she would do this to me?" He keeps looking to his watch, asking aloud, "What time is it?" Again, he looks down the hallway and then back to his watch, like he's waiting for an answer. "Damn, what time is it?" He sees the 'Exit' door. The answer is clear. "That's what time it is."

He runs to the door, but cracks it open slowly. He shoves his head into the opening like he's trying to squeeze his eyeball to the other side. He doesn't see anything. Leaning his ear on the door, he listens for footsteps. He doesn't hear anything, either.

He eases his tall, dark frame into the stairway. He remains paranoid like he's hearing voices, but he's only trying to figure out where to go. He moves over to the rail and cautiously peers below.

He sees it. It's a shadow, rushing up the staircase, in a circular motion. It's hauling ass.

Rell's chest is pounding so hard he can barely hear anything around him. He's breathing like a person who's having an asthma attack. He's so frightened that he's wheezing as he struggles to catch his breath. The last thing he needs is for his children's father to be locked away for the rest of his life, or even worse to be executed, for just trying to protect a friend who was attacked by a drunk cop.

The shadow in the stairway slows its pace. Rell holds his breath. He remains motionless, waiting to see what happens. The shadow comes to a complete stop.

Rell doesn't even realize that he's no longer breathing. He's spell bound. Literally, his mind is trapped in another world – a world of pain, fear, misery, and death.

The shadow is moving closer to the stair rail.

Rell sees the hand of the shadow rest on the rail below. He jumps back so quickly he hits the back of his head on the wall. He doesn't even pay attention to the knot that's growing on the back of his noggin. The pain is the last thing in the world he's concerned with. He needs to save his life right now.

He keeps his back to the wall as he leans forward to inspect the stairs above. It appears to be clear. Bending his knees, he slides down to the floor.

Rell wonders if the cop has seen him moving back. He knows the person looked up. And, if it was one of the cops, Rell should be running up the staircase now.

He thinks again. NOW! He scrambles up from his crouched position and crawls on his hands and knees up the stairs. Floor after floor, Rell doesn't slow down. Finally, he makes it to the top.

The roof door bursts open as Rell steps onto the roof. He takes only a couple steps forward before he surveys the entire area. All he sees is exhaust vents, air conditioner units, and a few storage rooms for equipment. Turning to his left, he almost walks into a large pigeon coop. The birds are startled. They're flapping wildly, flying and jumping all around the pen.

Moving away from the ruffled pigeons, he gives the roof a perimeter check. It's like he thought, he's trapped. He goes over to the edge and glimpses to the street. It's too far to fall, and he's scared of heights. He's fourteen stories up.

He thinks for a moment. "Maybe I could climb down to the window below me." He looks at the window again. "Hell nah, that's too far down."

Rechecking the roof, Rell sees that the space is fairly large. It has a lot of hiding places, but he doesn't want to take the chance of being caught by the police until he can at least speak with an attorney and his best friend Phillip.

Someone else ruffles the pigeons. Rell can hear them from the other side of the building. He crouches behind an air condition unit and spies on his new visitor. The person is on the other side of the pigeon pen.

Rell eases from one corner of the AC unit to the other corner in order to get a better view. He's stunned by the sight of his gunman. He's wearing a black ski mask, black gloves, black coat, black pants, and black boots – and he's definitely not a SWAT member or any kind of police officer. He's most definitely an assassin. It's obvious that his only job is to kill.

Rell's legs weaken as he slumps down. "Oh God, please help me." He re-inspects the roof as he whispers. "Please God, I need a way."

The pigeons are startled for a third time. Rell inches back up, revealing only the whiteness of his eyes. He sees another gunman. They're not talking, they're only giving one another hand signals. It only takes a couple seconds for their target to see the leader use his thumb as a knife to cut across his throat, indicating that he wants his men to kill the target. It officially sinks in to Rell that he is the one they want to kill.

Turning back around, he rests his back on the air unit. Looking across to the next building, Rell guesses it's about twenty feet apart from his building, and it's also a bit shorter in height. He checks the ground. He has about forty feet of running distance between him and the end of the roof.

Cocking his neck back, he flips around to see where his assassins are. It's good. They're checking the other direction. Without a second guess, Rell runs for the other building. He doesn't use his "back in the day confidence" he had when he used to run track and field in school. He uses all of the fear he has of losing his life and family, and all of the love he has for his family, to run with all of his might. He starts off slow, but he quickly gains ground as he sprints to the edge of the building. Within three feet of the drop-off, he attempts his jump to the next building.

While air born, his entire life flashes before his eyes. He thinks of his children, Tyra and Trevon. He thinks of his wife, Sheila. His friends, his good as well as his bad deeds. His feet land on the other roof top, but he falls over and slams into a small exhaust vent. His ribs hurt, but overall, he's fine.

Staggering to his feet, he quickly falls back down. He can't breathe. The vent has knocked the wind out of him. He rolls over and crawls to a hiding place behind a small chimney.

"My phone, my phone." He thinks the worse before retrieving it from his pocket. Checking it out, he realizes that the screen is cracked. Pressing the button to call his wife, he listens eagerly for the ringing sound. Thankfully, it's working, but still no answer from Sheila. He turns the phone off.

The weight of the world, suddenly, rests on his shoulders. His mind can't take it any longer. Tears begin to pattern his face. It's too much. He sobs as he slouches to the ground. His wife has betrayed him. He's wanted for the murder of a police officer. Two of his best friends have died. And now he has some strange assassins, who are not that far away, trying to kill him.

However, the thing that hurts him most is the fact that Sheila would betray him at a time like this; when he needs her most. How could she help them when she has to know that he wouldn't kill any man in cold blood? She knows that he would only do harm to man in self-defense.

Someone is cursing aloud. Rell hears it. He freezes into stone immediately. He listens, but the rest is unclear.

They must be close. He thinks.

He's terrified of losing his life. This makes him more cautious about making any foolish acts. He ponders very hard for a half of a second. He rotates his frame slowly as he tilts over to eavesdrop on his suspected assassins. He rests his eye right the side edge of the chimney. He can see them.

One is upset. He's waving his arms around like he's really pissed off. The other is trying to ease the unruly partner. The partner keeps yelling different curse words as he pulls away. Finally, another man runs to the pair and says something to the leader. The three begin to smile with pleasure. The leader pats his messenger on the back as they all walk away.

Plopping back down behind the chimney, Rell thinks to himself. "What the hell was that all about? Hmm, I must be too paranoid... They couldn't have been looking for me. They had to be here for someone else, because they look like they were relieved before they left."

Turning on his phone again, he calls his wife. Still no answer. He mumbles, "Damn, c'mon Sheila, answer your damn phone."

As he represses her number, he thinks of the men in black. "Damn, I feel sorry for whoever those guys were after. I hope he turns out all right in the end..." Wait, she probably didn't even bring her phone.

He gets up and goes to the edge of the roof. He wants to make sure that those thugs leave before he goes back over to Phillip's place. Sheila should be waiting.

After a few minutes, one of the men walks out from the entrance. Rell is anxiously waiting. Another man exits the apartment building. They're each going to separate cars. The first man had his car running and is already making a U-turn to the opposite side of the road. The second driver does the same. They stop in front of the entrance.

Rell is jittery with apprehensive thoughts. He wants to see who they are bringing out. He becomes antsy with anticipation.

The two drivers climb from their vehicles, walk around to the opposite side, and open the front passenger doors and the rear passenger doors.

Two more trenches exit the building. They stand by the car doors. None of them are wearing their masks any longer, but Rell still can't see their faces from so far above.

Another man is coming out. He has someone in a choke hold. These guys are serious. They don't care if it's daylight or not. They don't care about the couple of witnesses that are driving pass, but it doesn't even look like they even noticed the Henchmen.

Inching up higher over the edge, Rell watches them as they drag their hostage to the car. He takes a closer look – it's a woman. It's a black woman. He inspects a little closer... OH, SHIT!! It's Sheila. He jumps to his feet.

They slam her into the car. "Shit, what's the plate number?" He thinks for a second. He tries to cipher it from above. Before getting it, they pull off. Rell can no longer feel anything for himself. His whole world was just thrown into the back seat of a car with some killers. Yanking his phone from his pocket, he dials nine-one-one.

Fear is not an issue anymore. If he could fly, he would've jumped from the building to save his wife's life.

The phone is still ringing. He tries to remember all of the descriptions from the cars. The line is still ringing.

All of his nightmares have come true. Those men have taken one of the most precious things in his world from him, his wife. He can think of nothing right now, but Sheila. He watches the cars as they drive all the way down the street. He thinks, "This can't be happening – this is not real."

The operator finally answers the line. "Yes, this is 911. How can I help you?"

"Yes, I need to report a kidnapping. My wife..."

"Sir, did you say, 'A kidnapping?'"

"Yes, my wife has just been kidnapped by some men in a grey Dodge Charger." He gives the location.

"Sir, where did this take place?"

He loses his cool. "Bitch! Stop asking me so many questions! My wife is in a gray Dodge Charger. I think it's a 2017 model. There are two cars, but she's in the Dodge Charger. These men have a lot of guns. They just snatched her and threw her in their car." He watches the car disappear in the traffic. "Oh God, please send the police. These men might kill her!" His legs become weak at the thought of losing his wife. "Please, just send the police. My wife may die. Please, they're driving down 17th Street."

Chapter Ten

Big Joe enters his cubicle. He sets his lunch on his desk. He's tired. He didn't get much sleep last night.

Kicking his feet up on the desk, Tom smiles. "Hey big fella, good morning."

The big groggy guy glimpses to his left. "Oh hey partner, I didn't see you there." He reaches into one of his bags and pulls out a large cup. "Here, I brought us some coffee this morning." Tom attempts to grab it, but Joe withdraws it as he takes another one from the bag. "Wait, I gotta make sure you don't get mine. Mine is extra strong." He inspects the three cups, and he passes one to his partner.

Tom grabs the coffee. "Thanks, big guy." He smirks. "Now, I don't have to steal yours."

Joe reaches for the cup. "Give me that back."

Tom beats him by a split second and makes it out of his friend's reach. "No sir, I need this." He chuckles. "I'll treat tomorrow."

Getting a better look of his partner. "Hey, what's up with the new suit?"

Tom is wearing a new gray wool suit with a black tie and a crisp white shirt.

"Me and my ex have decided to go out tonight."

"What?"

"Yes, we've decided to try it one more time."

Big Joe drops his cup by accident. He rushes over to his partner, "I know you're only playing, right?"

Tom gives him a boyish grin. "No, I'm serious."

"And you do remember your last alcohol episode?" Joe growls, "Yes, I'm talking about your drinking problem."

Someone stops at their cubicle and clears their throat. The two Internal Affairs officers stop in the middle of their argument and turn to their new guest.

The visitor is wearing a pair of tan Dickies pants, a maroon button down, and a black leather jacket.

He adjusts his shades. "Uh, excuse me. I'm Detective Ryan Brewkowski. I'm here to see Detectives Joseph Brown and Tom Riley."

The two detectives first look to each other and give a vindictive stare before turning back to their new guest and replacing the frowns with fake smiles.

Joe extends his arm to shake Brewkowski's hand. "Yes, we've been waiting for you." He cuts his eye back at his partner, letting him know that they will definitely finish their discussion later. "Uh, give us a moment and we'll go somewhere where we can sit and talk privately."

Tom doesn't want to remain in the office with his partner, so he leaves with detective Brewkowski. "Don't worry. I'll take him to one of the private rooms in the back."

It takes less than two minutes for the trio to reach the small room at the rear of the building. Tom opens the door and turns on the light before asking detective Brewkowski to take a seat at a plain, pale, old gray table.

The room is plain and simple. Its walls are crispy white. It's small and tight, barely larger than a small bathroom. There's a small camera in the corner of one wall, aimed directly at Brewkowski's position.

Tom grabs one of the two black government chairs on his side and takes a seat across from the guest. He doesn't waste any time. "You know why you're here, don't you?"

Brewkowski replies. "I'm assuming you're just following the typical protocol for a murdered officer's partner."

Tom and Big Joe are still frowning at one another. The feisty Irish takes his cup from the table and smiles sarcastically, "Why, thank you partner." Tom says, taking a sip. "You're the greatest."

Ignoring his smart-ass partner, Joe sits beside the deceased's partner while pushing over a cup of coffee. "Okay. Detective Brewkowski, do you understand why you're here?"

"Yes, your partner has already explained it to me." He's only been here for a few minutes and he's already ready to go. "Would you guys like me to tell you about that night?"

Looking at each other first, the I.A. detectives then turn to him and nod their heads at the same time.

Clasping his hands together, Brewkowski rests his elbows on the wobbly table. "We were there for this B and E perp who's been tearing the area apart..."

"Hold up!" Joe is waving his hand for Brewkowski to stop. "I must inform you that you are being recorded, and everything you say can be used against you."

He nods to the warning. "I know my rights and that everything is being recorded. Don't forget I work for the law enforcement, too." Inspecting the two interrogators with a suspicious eye, he goes on. "Now, would you like me to continue?"

Joe drops his hand. "Guh-head, you may continue."

"Well then," Brewkowski says, taking a sip of his new-found coffee. "Man, this stuff is great. What's in it?"

Smiling from ear to ear, the big guy blushes. "Well, I can't tell you, but one of my secret ingredients is a little mint chocolate."

Cutting in on the two, Tom gets back to business. "Listen, detective Brewkowski, I'm happy to hear that you enjoy the taste of my partner's coffee, but right now we have a very serious issue at hand."

"Uh yes, I apologize for that. It's just that I've been going through a lot every since the incident. My therapist has instructed me to work on looking at the good things in life and not dwell on the bad."

"Hmm," Tom thinks, twisting his lips. "Whatever the case - could you please tell us about the night of the murder of your partner, Marten O'Brien?"

Brewkowski takes another drink of his coffee as he spends over thirty minutes explaining everything that happened the night of his partner's demise. He tells them about the areas burglary issues. He informs them that his partner was acting drunk to draw out the burglar. He even sobs from time to time when he discusses the acts that were closer to his partner's death. In the end, he describes how his partner slowly dropped to the pavement, in front of him, and how he wasn't able to do anything about it.

He pounds the table with anger and frustration. "I couldn't save my own damn friend!" He looks up to his interrogators. "I couldn't do anything!"

Tom and Joe give their visitor a moment to calm down and get himself together. They don't leave the room; they just sit there and watch him as he cries.

It doesn't take much longer for the feisty Irish to interrupt the detective's emotional moment. "Could you tell me, again, what you saw from your car?"

Joe hands him some tissue.

He nods as he wipes his face. "I was sitting in my car waiting for him to radio in. His line was quiet for twenty minutes."

Tom interrupts. "Twenty minutes?"

"Yes, that is what we agreed to. We didn't want anyone to see him talking on a phone, a mic, or anything else. He was supposed to appear to be a drunk."

Tom keeps him going. "Okay, you can finish from where you left off."

"After the twenty minutes passed, I was beginning to get a little worried until he radioed in."

Tom leans forward. "What did he say?"

"He only said that he was headed my way." Brewkowski waits for another question, but the I.A. detectives only stare at him for more information. "I then waited for him. I waited patiently, until I seen the shapes of what I thought to be a bunch of thugs fighting in the middle of the ally."

"Why did you think they were thugs?" The big I.A. detective is curious.

"I thought they were thugs because it was a large group of them, and our perp is only one man."

Tom rests his chin in his palms as he leans on the table. "So, what type of thugs did you think they were for you not to intervene? And why didn't you radio your partner to warn him about anything out of the ordinary?" Things just aren't adding up.

"Uh, I didn't want to jeopardize the stake-out." Brewkowski's eyes jump back and forth between the I.A. detectives. "I mean. . . you know how it is when you don't want to give up your cover."

The word "cover" seems to be the key term at the moment.

Tom laughs. "And why didn't you radio your partner?"

Brewkowski appears frustrated. "I told you already. We were trying to keep the air waves quiet."

Scratching his forehead, Big Joe leans back. "I think my partner, Detective Riley, asked you what type of thugs did you think they were – but you never answered." His eyes are probing Brewkowski. "What type of thugs did you think they were, for you not to want to assist, in any way?"

Shaking his index finger, Brewkowski stands to his feet. "Uh-uh! Oh no!" He looks down to his interrogators with the taste of venom in his mouth. "You bastards are not about to say that this is some form of racism that cost my partner to lose his life! Those thugs killed him in cold blood!"

Joe jumps to his feet. "You're exactly right! We're not going to say it was some form of racism, because you paid those bastards to kill O'Brien- in cold blood!"

Plopping down in his chair, Brewkowski seems confused. "What? "But, why would I do that?"

Joe's hulking frame leans over the table. "Because you were having an affair with his wife."

"What? What did she say to you people?"

Tom jumps back in. "Ryan-wait, would you mind if I call you Ryan?"

Brewkowski shakes his head. "No... . No, I don't mind."

"Well, Ryan. Could you please tell the two of us why your partner's blood alcohol level was so high? The test states that he had enough in him to piss a hundred and eighty proof." He rises from his chair. "Or... could you please tell us why on the night of the homicide, you reeked of liquor?"

Big Joe walks around the table. "You know the video tape is almost finished?"

Brewkowski stands up and backs to the wall. "No, I didn't know that. But what does it have to do with me?"

Joe grins. "You're going to jail."

Reaching for the door knob, Brewkowski wises up. "I don't want to go any further. I want my lawyer."

Tom eases closer. "Good, who's your lawyer?"

"I don't have one, yet, but I'll let him talk to you when I get one."

Joe is directly in front of him. "You can leave now!" Before Ryan moves an inch, Big Joe grabs his shoulder. "But remember, he who snitches first is the lottery winner. You don't have much time before we lock you and that whore of a widow up for the rest of your lives."

Pulling away from him, the anger appears on Brewkowski's face. "I want a fucking lawyer. Get your damn hands off of me."

Chapter Eleven

A lot of time has elapsed. It took Rell over an hour to get off of the roof. He had to beat on the door for an hour and ten minutes before a child heard the banging and responded to his aid. It took another fifteen minutes for him to convince the little boy to open the door for him and allow him in.

Crossing from building to building was almost as difficult. He had to make it past all of the residents without being seen. For the first time in his life, he realized how many people really live in his friends' neighborhood. Every corner he turned, he saw people hanging out, working, or just being plain ole nosy and watching everyone passing by.

Impatiently, he waits behind a dumpster at the rear of Phillip's apartment building. He's sweating with fear in his heart. He's trembling with worry for his wife's life. His body and mind are aching from sleep deprivation.

Someone is exiting the back door. It's an old white lady with a cocker spaniel in her arms. As she steps through, she sets her dog on the ground.

"Dere you go Poo-Poo. Mommy is watching you."

Rell, steps from behind the dumpster before she sees him, and acts like he was throwing out some trash. "How are you doing, ma'am?" he asks the elderly lady.

She's startled. "Oh dear, I didn't see you sonny." Fixing her round glasses, she responds to his inquiry. "I'm doing fine, dear."

As he approaches her, he tries to adjust his clothes properly. "Whew, the weather is feeling great today."

As their gap closes, the grandmother leans forward as she glares at him narrowly, pressing her glasses against the bridge of her nose.

She pokes her index finger at him. "I... I've seen your face somewhere."

He stumbles over his own foot. "Huh?"

She's right in front of him now. She looks his face over. "Yes, I've seen you on TV." Leaning away, she squints from one eye. "What's your name, sonny?"

Rell's mouth drops to the floor. He doesn't move. He only stands there, staring at her face to face.

Quickly, he sizes her up as he thinks to himself. "Should I knock her ass out and throw her in the dumpster behind me?" He peers down to the dog. "Damn, I'll have to do something with this mutt, too." He clenches his fist as he raises his head.

She places her hands on her hips. "Now sonny, I'm not going to ask you but one more time... what's your name?"

Lifting his arm, he begins to say something.

She's quicker. She raises her tiny fist and holds it back, preparing for a furious blow to his chest.

Rell caughs as he rests a palm on her shoulder. "Ma'am..." looking around. "Ma'am, my name is Taye Diggs. I'm an actor. You've probably seen me on many movies and TV shows."

Raising her glasses, she agrees. "I knew you were a movie star. You're built just like one of those handsome stallions from Hollywood."

He places his finger in front of his lips. "Shhh, but please don't let people know that I live here in the building now."

She slightly ducks, like someone can hear the two of them. "Yes, you're right. I mean, I won't tell a soul."

He smiles from ear to ear. "Thank you."

Smiling bashfully, she asks a favor. "But can I get your autograph, please?"

Checking his pockets, he comes up empty handed. "I would, but I don't have a pen."

Stepping back in the door, she talks to her dog. "Come in, Poo-Poo. We have to get a pen for the big Hollywood actor." As the dog jumps to her hands, she pulls the pup in. "His name is Taye Diggs."

Sneaking through the building like he had the one adjacent to it, he makes it to Phillip's first apartment floor. It's obvious the gunmen were here, because all of the lights on the floor have been broken, leaving the hallway pretty dark. There's only a little light emitting through the window at the end of the hall.

Rell waits and listens for any kind of movement. He doesn't want to take any chances on being caught by any remaining gunmen or any of the city police – he definitely needs to know what's going on.

After standing in the door for a while, he runs for his friend's apartment. At the door, he realizes that it's open. He walks in. The place is in shambles. A lot of the furniture has been turned over. Lamps are broken. Their shattered glass is all over the floor.

Two steps in, he stops in his tracks. He looks to the floor; it's stained from splattered blood on some of the broken glass. His heart can't take anymore.

Someone comes in from his rear. It's a woman. "What in the world!" she yells.

The woman startles Rell. He whips his neck around with lightning speed. "Whoa! You startled me." It's Phillip's wife. "Wanda, I didn't hear you come in behind me."

"Terrell, what's going on here and where is my husband?" Pushing pass him, she starts hollering for Phillip. "Phillip! Get out here, we need to talk!"

Running behind her, Rell grabs her by the arm. "Wait... when was the last time you saw him?"

"He's not with you?" she asks. Rell feels the fear creep up his spine.

"No, I'm by myself. I was waiting for Sheila, but she was kidnapped."

"Wha... Kidnapped?" Tearing away, she snatches her phone out. "I'm calling the police."

"No." He takes her phone. "Listen to me." Standing back, she gives him an oh-no you didn't take my phone from me stare. He holds his two palms up. "Wait a second. I'm not trying to piss you off. I just want to know whatever you know, so that I can get to the bottom of this." Dropping his hands. "I've been waiting to hear from Phillip for over a week. He had me waiting upstairs at the other apartment." She tries to say something, but he stops her. "My wife called me. We talked and decided that she would come over and meet me here. . .. Once she got here, a group of men came in with a bunch of guns and kidnapped her." He sits down on the couch. "I need to know what's going on."

She takes a good look at him for a moment and then she bows her head. Sheila whispers, "Please, close the door." Without a second thought, Rell jumps up and closes the door. He sits back down before she can get another word out. She faces him. "What I'm about to tell you, you can tell no one – not even Sheila."

Shaking his head, he promises. "No, I won't tell anyone."

"My husband was doing some work on the side, because we wanted to purchase a home somewhere on the outskirts of the city."

Softly rubbing her shoulder, he tries to ease her nerves. "Okay...".

"There was some company in New York that wanted to contract an architect. It wanted bids to do drawings for some building in Harlem." Tears begin to drip from her eyes. "He won the bid because you know how he hates to lose anything, so he gave the lowest possible bid and got the contract."

Rell remains calm and quiet, but he's really anxious to leave and get somewhere safe. "It's okay, Wanda, you can tell me more."

"It was the Italian Mafia." She gives a heavy sob. "They wanted him to back out of the deal, because they had already had someone who was supposed to win the contract."

He coughs. "Oh, shit!"

"They threatened to kill him if he didn't back down, but you know how he is – he can be very hard headed." Wiping her face, she broke the news. "I think they have Sheila. They probably think she's me."

Continuing to speak, Rell stops her again. "Wait Wanda, let me think; this is too much for one man right now."

The weight of the world seems to be on his shoulders. Reyquan and Carlos died in his car. He's wanted for the murder of a cop. His wife has been kidnapped by the Mafia. His friend, Phillip, is missing and may possibly be in the hands of the Mafia, too.

Who knows what the mob may be doing to his wife. Or to Phillip. They may be torturing the two.

Just the thought by itself causes him to swallow a big lump in his throat. He taps Phillip's wife's knee. "Listen, I need you to go buy me a pre-paid phone – and I need it now." As she heads for the door, he adds to the order. "And make sure you get me a lot of minutes."

After she closes the door behind her, he thinks of the police being after him. Now that his photo is displayed all over the television, it won't be long before people start calling in with his name and information. He rechecks his phone to make sure it's turned off. He knows the police will be checking for his last location of a call, so he definitely doesn't have much time to spare. He has to get the hell out of dodge and now.

Checking the clock, thirty minutes have passed since Sheila left and it seems like a week. Still, Rell doesn't know what to do or how to go about it. He has the world after him for the murder of a cop, and he must figure out how to do battle with the underworld in order to get his wife and friend back. He feels like a kitten being chased by a German Shepherd but has to fight a hungry Pit Bull in order to live.

As soon as Wanda returns, a thought pops into his mind. "Please, tell me you have the phone."

Hurriedly, she reaches in the bag. "Yes. I got you two," she says, giving him one pack and setting the other on the broken night stand. "I also got you over a thousand minutes for each one."

Rell immediately starts texting someone. He presses SEND and texts the person again a couple more times.

Phillip's wife sits there waiting for him to say something, but he doesn't. Leaning in, she finally asks." Who are you calling?'"

"Your husband and I..." The prepaid starts ringing. He taps the SEND button and places the phone against his ear. "Yeah." Wanda tries to eavesdrop, but she can't hear who's on the other end. He continues to talk. "Something very bad is happening." He looks around. "Wait, a lot of bad things are happening, and I really need your help." The line becomes silent. "Good. I'm at Phillip's place, and I need you to get here like last week." He's quiet again. "Alright, call me at this number when you're near."

She watches him end the call. "Who was that?"

He places the phone in his pocket. "That's my last resort." He picks her hand up and gives her a sincere touch. "I need you to go to a girlfriend's house or a coworker's place and lay low for a while."

"What? Wait. I don't have anyone. You know I am not from here."

"Well then, take a leave of absence and go back down to Georgia because things are about to get dangerous here, and it'll probably never be the same."

A tear lands on her cheek. "Just bring my husband back."

"I will. . ." He checks his watch. "I also need you to go get your son and my children and take them with you to Georgia." Gripping her hands tighter, he continues. "If I don't make it out of this, please let them know that their parents love them."

Chapter Twelve

It's at the end of their working day, and the two are still going over the facts of the case. They haven't left the interrogation room, yet. They needed the privacy to help keep their minds clear of any distractions.

Since Detective Brewkowski left, the pair has been through what seems like a hundred cups of coffee and various munchies, including chocolate chip cookies, potato chips, and Snicker's candy bars.

Biting into his Chips Ahoy chocolate chip cookie, Tom chews fast as he speaks with his hand over his mouth. "Okay, let's say that he was only acting like he was drunk that night. . ." Taken another big bite, he finishes his train of thought. "I've been drunk many times and you and I both know that mostly all drunks talk or mumble when they're drunk." Reaching back into the bag, he poses a familiar question. "And why did he need the alcohol?" Not giving his partner a chance to speak, he jumps to a new thought. "Wait, we need to bring in every officer that was on that scene that night and apply a little pressure on them to find out why no one filed a complaint on Brewkowski for drinking while on duty."

After listening to his partner ramble for a few minutes, Joe turns back to his lap top and presses play again. "You see. Look at that." He pushes the pause button. "You see, right there." "Do you see the fear in his eyes?" Joe asks, pointing to the killer's face.

The FBI and the special forensic team did extremely well with the video clips. It's so clear; you can actually see the water beading down the murderer's cheeks.

Tapping the screen, Joe keeps talking. "Tom, he's terrified. Something is not right." Rewinding the video, Joe searches for one more thing to show Tom. "I have something else I want you to see." Joe finds what he's looking for and pauses the clip. "Look at this, Tom."

On the video, a staggering man can be seen entering the ally.

Tom interjects, "That's O'Brien."

Joe shakes his head. "Mmm-hmmm."

The drunk staggers deeper into the ally before a man jumps him from his blind side and beats him to the ground. Afterwards, three men immediately enter the dark road.. One jumps in and separates the staggering drunk from the attacker.

Big Joe suddenly stops the video. "There . . .," he says, tapping Tom's forearm. "What's that?" Joe quickly rewinds the clip. "Look. Right there."

There it is. It's something shiny in O'Brien's hand, and he's poking it at the other man.

Tom leans closer. "It's a knife."

The two watch the entire match between the officer and the murderer. Through the entire sitting they do nothing but take notes. They each have over two pages of questions thus far, and they haven't even finished checking through half of the issues surrounding the case.

Finally, Tom can't take it anymore. Dropping his pad on the table, he finally lets it out. "Why in hell is O'Brien trying to stab him with a knife?" Standing up, he continues to vent. "And why is Brekowski claiming he couldn't do anything knowing that the camera was rolling?"

Someone knocks on the door. Tom is already standing, so he opens it and greets the person who was waiting on the other side. It's a woman; she hands him a computer printout and walks away.

Setting his pad down, Joe stretches back in his chair. "So, what does it say?"

Scanning the sheet, Tom gives a dazed expression. "You were right; there haven't been any B&E's in the area in over three months. Before that, it was six months and before that one it was four months before that... But, this leaves me more confused. Didn't he realize that we would check into all of this? Is he stupid or something?"

Joe sips more coffee. "Alright, these are some of the things I wrote down that I definitely want to check further into: The level of alcohol in his blood? The strange fight on the video? Marten's strange wife? Why Brewkowski couldn't see the scuffle? And most importantly, who was the guy who passed the wife the suspicious envelope?" Setting his cup back on the wobbling table, he remembers one more thing. "Oh, and why in the hell is O'Brien jumping on people in dark allies with a knife in his hand?"

Somebody is at the door again. They're pounding pretty hard.

Tom swings it open. "Yeah?"

It's a woman with a big beautiful smile. "I wanted to let you guys know that the suspect in the O'Brien case has been Identified, and they're about to have a live press meeting on television."

The partners run right past her.

Everyone is in the breaking area with both TVs turned all the way up. The crowd is huge, and every person is struggling to get closer to the tube. Tom gets behind his huge, muscular partner and follows his solid frame to the front of the on-lookers.

The pair missed some of the opening comments, but it wasn't of any importance. The mayor was only giving thanks to the forensic teams for making this possible. The mayor then turns around and calls Chief O'Connor to the podium.

Automatically, O'Connor cuts all of the small talk. "The suspect wanted for questioning is the man displayed on your screen." Immediately, Rell's photo appears on the TV screen. "His name is Terrell Jacobs. He is considered to be armed and dangerous. He is wanted for the murder of detective Marten O'Brien."

The reporters go into a frenzy and initiate a barrage of questions for the chief and/or whoever else that may be willing to answer them.

One reporter is holding her arm in the air. The chief points to her, and waits for her rehearsed question. "Chief O'Connor, our sources say that the accused killer is a loan manager for a local bank. What do you have to say to this?"

The chief scorches her with his eyes. "Ma'am, the occupation of an accused murderer is irrelevant in this homicide case."

Back at the Internal Affairs Office, they all think the same thing. "A banker?!"

Joe and his partner need not hear anymore. Their investigation just intensified. He and Tom break out of the crowd and head for their desks. They need all the information they can get on this Terrell Jacobs guy. There are a lot of questions that definitely need to be answered. The most important one still being why would a banker kill a cop?

Chapter Thirteen

Rell is too impatient to sit down. He's been pacing the floor ever since his last phone call to his mysterious friend. He walks over to the window, peeps between the blinds, and sees nothing.

His phone rings. He flips it open. "Hello." The person on the other side says a couple of words. "I'm on my way down," Rell tells caller.

It takes less than a split second for Rell to pull the door shut behind him, as he heads down to his rendezvous. He patiently retraces the same path he used coming up. Not much has changed. The same faces are still in the same places and, like the last time, they don't even see him as he passes them all.

He stops at the glass door of the rear entrance and glances through. There's a car idling by the dumpster. Stretching his neck back out, he sees the occupant of the car. It's a longtime friend, Supreme, from his childhood years.

Shaking his head, he mumbles. "A Bentley."

He's stunned. He can't believe that out of all he cars in the world to drive, his friend would choose to drive a Bentley Continental GT on a day when every cop on the planet is searching for him, and his wife and Phillip are in the hands of the Italian Mafia. This is the last thing he needs – to have every person they pass by staring at them and the car. So much for trying to go unnoticed. This is definitely not an inconspicuous ride.

The Bentley Gt is a stunner. It's a glossy, oily black on black with twenty-two inch chromed Avanti rims. Supreme always kept his ride plain and simple, but nonetheless an eye catcher to anyone that passes. This car exemplifies power and elegance all in one. It is the definition of simple chic, and the epitome of any car enthusiast's dream.

After checking for the fifteenth time to see that it was clear, Rell pushes the door open and runs to the car. The door opens as he approaches. Running around the door, he jumps into the car and slams it behind him.

Twisting his face, Supreme growls. "Hold up, don't be slamming my door. I know you got problems, but don't take anything out on any of my rides."

Rell slouches down in his seat to hide from anyone passing by. "Man, why did you have to drive this car?" He faces him, "A damn Bentley. Really?"

Putting the gear in reverse, Supreme doesn't get it. "What's wrong with my car?"

Rell raises his voice. "Supreme. . . I have every cop in the city after me... Then again, I'm probably already on America's Most Wanted."

Turning his stereo system down, Supreme gets serious. "Wait. Why would the police be after your square ass?"

Rell hunches lower in the seat. "I murdered a cop."

"YOU?" Supreme asks in confusion.

Rell tries to explain. "It was an accident. I was only defending myself. He was trying to kill me."

"For what? What did you do?" he asks Rell.

"I didn't do anything. He was drunk, and he attacked Carlos. I broke them up. He tried to stab me first, and then he grabbed for his gun..." A blankness comes over Rell's face. "I couldn't let him kill me, Supreme. I couldn't let him take me from my children." He pauses for a thought. "All I know, is he attacked me at the lounge. . ."

"All of this happened at a lounge?" Supreme asks.

"No, it started at the lounge, but ended in an alley."

Supreme turns on to Ocean Avenue as he listens to his friend's tale of horror and confusion. He's even shocked by how frightened Rell becomes every time he passes a pedestrian.

He's known Rell, Phillip, Reyquan, and Carlos all of his life. When they were kids they used to call themselves the Five Elements. As normal, things change as boys grow into men.

Supreme was raised in the projects by his single mother. At one time, his four best friends were all he had. He didn't know that his father was a very wealthy man who lived in Staten Island, just a borough away from Supreme's Brooklyn residence. By the time he found out that his father was a major real estate investor, Supreme was already a king pin in the drug game.

His father died young, and when he did, he left him over twenty brown stone homes and two apartment buildings. Supreme's father made sure that his son could be set for the rest of his life if he chose to. However, it was already too late. Supreme was already stuck in the game of street life.

They make a right on 13th Avenue.

With a nervous flinch, he thumps Supreme. "Hey, why are you getting on the turnpike?" Climbing over to the back seat, Rell starts to panic. "Are you trying to get me locked up? You know I might be seen when we go through the toll booth!"

"Listen, you just stay back there and be calm." Supreme watches him through the rearview mirror and gives a sincere glare. "You tell me, Rell... do you think that I would ever do anything to place you in any kind of harm?"

Rell doesn't get the opportunity to answer. They're approaching the toll area. Rell slides down to the floor of the vehicle and pulls his coat over his head.

The New Jersey turnpike is really busy right now; it's rush hour. There are thousands of drivers commuting to and from any of the many cities in the area. They could be going to Newark, Jersey City, Patterson, or other cities in New Jersey or New York, or even one of the up-state states like Connecticut. It's really packed like always, bumper to bumper.

As he pulls the car up to the booth, the lady doesn't smile or frown. She only chews her gum as she extends her arm out to pass him the toll booth ticket that shows where he got on the turnpike.

Glimpsing to the mirror, Supreme locates Rell. "Hey, it's clear. You can get up now."

He mumbles, "I'm fine down here. I don't want to get up until we get to where we are going."

Thirty minutes have passed. Rell awakens to a familiar lighting with a familiar hollow sound. It's the Holland Tunnel. He doesn't know why, but he smiles with joy. Even when he was only a little boy, he would always smile whenever he could smell New York City or even hear the sound of the cars as they ride through the Lincoln or Holland tunnels.

As soon as they hit Canal Street, Rell raises back up. "Whoa, why are you turning left? I thought you were going to take me to Brooklyn."

Driving up Hudson, Supreme confesses. "Nah, I can't take you to my place right now. Things are not going so good for me either."

"What's wrong?" Rell is genuinely concerned about his childhood pal.

"Don't worry about what's wrong with me. I need to get you out of this country before we start worrying about me."

"C'mon man, tell me what's wrong with you?"

Supreme checks the mirror to find his friend staring back at him from the back seat. "Something happened to one of my friends" Supreme says.

"You mean one of your business friends?" Rell asks.

"Yes, his name is Czar."

"You talking about that Dominican guy?" Rell is trying to put a face to the name.

"Yes and no. Yes, that's the dude, but he's not Dominican decent. He's half black and half Mexican." Resting his foot on the brake pedal, Supreme tries to help Rell remember Czar. "You remember...he's the cat who came to your bank with me that time when your old Toyota Celica was in the shop having to get fixed for the thousandth time." He grins.

"Okay, yeah. I remember him. Now, what's going on? Rell is familiar with name now and wants to know what happened.

Supreme gives it a second thought, but reminds himself that he just had all of his cars checked for bugs the other day. Peering to his left as he approaches Abingdon Square, he heads up Eighth Avenue and thinks twice about talking to his friend about something so serious.

Turning back to the mirror, he's honest with Rell. "I shouldn't be telling you this, so don't expect to hear much."

"Okay." Rell replies as he tiredly stares back.

"Well. . ." Pausing as he gives his ole best friend a quizzical nod. "My friend, Czar, ran into some major problems with the law down in Richmond, Virginia. He's in jail awaiting murder and drug trafficking charges."

"You're saying that you think he'll snitch?"

"NO!" Supreme frowns as he slows the car. "No, I'm not worried about Czar snitching. I'm worried about what his snitch said about the whole set up." Applying pressure to the gas, he continues the story. "I didn't even know that he was locked up. He told some Spanish cat named El Monstro to tell me about everything and to close shop."

"So, you're alright?" Rell isn't sure what this really has to do with Supreme.

"No. There was this guy, KOB, who told on everything that he could think of, and this bastard knew that I was buying from Czar, too." Looking up to the Brazil Grill ahead, Supreme seems worried. "Right now, no one can take any chances, and I'll be leaving after I get you outta here, first."

"Where are you sending me?" Rell wants to know.

Supreme says, "I'll see if I can send you to Mexico, where I'm going. From there, I'll get you to Cuba."

"But, wait, you're going to Cuba, too?" Rell is getting more confused and has a million things going through his mind at the moment.

Supreme answers, "If things turn bad, yes. If they don't, then I'll come back here."

Supreme takes Rell to one of his Harlem hideouts. Getting there wasn't the problem. Finding a good parking place, however, proved to be very different. After making a couple phone calls, a few young men came out of their apartments and moved their vehicles.

Getting off the elevator on the tenth floor, Supreme hands his ole pal the apartment key and points to the door three apartments down to the right.

Supreme points towards the door. "Guh-head, I'm right behind you." The elevator doors are closing. "Just go in and have a seat. I have to run back down to handle something."

Rell slides the key in the hole and turns it before twisting the knob. He's nervous. Once inside, he leaves the door cracked and checks the place out to make sure everything is safe. He goes in all three bedrooms. He checks the den, the living room, the kitchen, and even the fire escape. Everything appears to be good.

Picking up the remote control, he plops down on the couch and turns on the television. The screen quickly clears to show a beautiful woman sitting on the edge of the bed with her legs spread wide open. She's wearing a red gartered slip made with a stretched satin fish net design. Her G-string and crisscross-topped, sheer thigh high spandex are all fitting her like a glove.

Her complexion is as pale as porcelain, but her ivory skin still looks soft and creamy. She's speaking so soft; Rell can barely understand a word. He presses the plus sign on the volume button and holds it until he can hear what she's saying.

He sits back. He can tell she's German by her strong accent. She pronounces her w's like v's.

Wait, she's pushing her panties to the side with one hand as she eases a finger in between her beautiful pink folds of womanhood. She's talking to someone. She's asking them what they want.

Another woman walks into the frame of the camera. She is just as beautiful, but her skin is the polar opposite of the first woman. Her skin is a dark, rich, cocoa hue and her body is spectacular. Just like the German female, her hair is long. She's wearing a twig colored, patterned, mesh bustier top. It has a laced-up front, and the sides have detachable garters that are holding her sheer stockings in their proper position. To top it off,

133

she's wearing a matching pair of mesh crotchless panties.

A grin appears on Rell's face as he watches the blue-eyed blonde and the curvaceous black women embrace one another with a passionate kiss. He looks to the door to make sure he locked it.

The black woman climbs to the bed and sits behind the German woman. The brunette draws out a silver dildo and places it at the tip of her lover's lips. The blonde immediately licks the tip of it, and then leans forward to suck on the tip of it.

After a moment, the brunette slides the toy down to her girlfriend's warm, wet opening and slowly pushes it inside. The two are moaning as they begin to please one another. Suddenly, a man walks into the picture. His back is turned to the camera; he can only be seen from the waist down. He's wearing a black trench. That part seems a little odd.

The man in the coat rests his palms on is waist as he watches the two sexy women make love to each other. The blonde sees him and pushes the toy away from her hot, throbbing spot.

She pouts her lips. "Darling, I vaunt you to hurt my pussy." She smiles. "If you don't hurt my pussy, I'll be very upset."

Opening his coat, he surprises her with an enormous hard on. She moves in front of him as he strokes himself, waiting for him to place the head of his penis in her warm, waiting mouth. His muscular, golden, mahogany frame towers over the two of them.

The ivory woman and the man fall back onto the bed, and she props her knees up. He grabs her by her calves and pulls her hour glass frame to the edge of the bed. He doesn't play like he's in some romance book; he plunges the head of his stiff rod into her dripping entrance and starts to pound her.

She's giving orgasmic gestures with her tongue as she rolls it around in her mouth. He grabs her thighs and uses them as his handles to ram her against his shaft. Her juices are flowing with every hit, and he's not trying to slow down.

A cold sweat appears on Rell's face as he watches. He's really aroused. He looks over to check the door again, and then eases his hand down into his britches.

Now, the brunette climbs from behind the two love birds. Her body is so smooth. Her skin looks like creamy, sweet chocolate. Her rear end is perfectly sized and toned. Her waist is tiny. Her lips are small and pursed together, like she's about to pout.

She pushes him back, and she lays down on top of her German dime-piece. The two women begin to tongue one another as the man walks out of the camera frame.

The blonde wraps her legs around her sexy friend as they enjoy their passionate moment.

Rell begins to grip himself tight. He works his hand up and down. He licks his lips as he dreams of being able to taste the wetness of both of the women he's been watching.

The man walks back into the picture. Once again, his back is to the camera. He drops his trench. He has a strap-on dildo around his lower waist.

Grabbing the chocolate skinned woman, he rolls the two of them over so that the blonde is on top and the brunette is at the bottom. He pushes his dick into his chocolate candy treat as he pushes the dildo into the German bombshell. The two women begin to scream and cry out in ecstasy. He's pounding away. Cum is slowly dripping down the thigh of the blonde. It drips all the way down to the brunette's leg. With her index finger, the brunette runs the length of her leg until she feels the warm fluid. She takes her cum covered finger and traces her lips as if putting on lipstick. The blonde turns to her and licks the excess from her lover's lips.

Rell can't take anymore. He unzips his pants and pulls his penis out. He's stroking as fast as he possibly can.

Someone walks in the room. "Vutt are you doing!" The woman walks in front of him and turns off the television.

His eyes are wide open. He shoves his penis back into his pants and zips them back up. "Huh?"

"I said, vutt are you doing, you pervert?"

He takes a good look at the woman; somehow it really is the German female from the movie. "Huh? I didn't know." Rell is so confused about what just happened.

She runs out of the room.

Supreme comes in. "Hey man, how are you feeling?"

Rell is slightly tongue tied at the moment. "I'm do-do-ing..." he looks over his shoulders. "Uh, Preme, I think I messed up."

Supreme tries to console him. "C'mon man, don't worry. We'll get through this."

"Uh, I'm not talking about the other stuff." Rell doesn't even know where to begin now.

The blonde walks back into the room with the brunette from the video. "That's the sick bastard." Pointing at him, she walks closer. "He vuss masturbating to our movie."

Rell, shakes his head as he thinks to himself: Well, that's one way to tell Supreme what just happened. Turning to the women, He tries to explain. "I didn't know it was a home video."

The two women stand behind their man as if they are trying to hide their bodies from Rell's view.

The brunette speaks softly. "Supreme, do something. Have him beaten or something."

Lifting his arms to the air, he tries to comfort her. "Hold up baby, I'm not going to have him beaten." He turns around to face his ladies. "You two just calm down and have a seat on the stools." He points at the stools by the entrance to the den. "Rell, what happened while I was gone?"

"Look, I made a mistake. I just came in and turned the TV on, and that video started playing." He stands up and realizes the movie is still playing. He turns it off. "I didn't know that it was a home movie."

The long-haired black female yells from the stool. "So you just come and play with yourself in anybody's house?"

"Noooooo, I didn't know that anyone stayed here." Looking to his longtime pal, he pleaded for help in the matter. "Tell them Preme. You didn't tell me anything; you just said to make myself at home." Folding his arms in defense, Rell continues. "I thought you two were porn stars or something."

The two women jump up. "PORN STARS!"

Supreme laughs. "You two calm down. No Rell, they're not porn stars. One is a stock broker and the other is a lawyer. Well, actually, she was a law student in Germany, but she will have her law degree here in two more months." He turns back to his ladies. "Okay my loves, it was a harmless mistake. He didn't know. It was all my fault and I apologize."

The two women get up, walk over to the television, and completely disconnect the DVR. They pout their lips as they take it with them.

Supreme and Rell watch the two as they head for the door. They slam it behind them.

Rell gives a deep sigh. "Damn man, I'm sorry. I didn't mean to get you in any trouble." Rell rubs the sweat from his face. "You have two women?"

"Well no, I don't have two. I only have one, the black girl, but the white girl is her girlfriend and I guess we all like to have a little fun. And don't worry, I'm not in trouble."

"But they left," Rell reminds.

"Nah, we were leaving anyway. We're all going upstairs until you're in a safe location." Standing over his friend, he explains why he left him alone. "I figured you'd need a little time to go over everything that's happening."

Pulling his pre-paid phone out, Rell nods his head. "Yeah, I do need some time to handle a few things before I even think about leaving this country."

Supreme reaches out to stop him. "Wait, who are you calling?"

Shaking his head, Rell tells him what he's doing. "Don't worry, this is a pre-paid and I'm checking on Tyra and Trevon."

"Where are they? I'll send someone over to pick them up."

"Don't worry; they're with Phillip's wife, Wanda."

The call goes through. It's answered on the second ring. A woman's soft voice says hello.

"Wanda, it's me. Are you safe?"

"Yes, I have the kids and we're on the turnpike right now."

"You're driving all the way down?"

"Yes, I don't want to take any chances. I got the preacher from my church to get me a rent-a-car. No one even knows that I left the city."

"That's good. Are the kids awake?"

"Yeah, they're up. Here goes Tyra." She passes Tyra the phone.

Her throat crackles as her moping voice hits the phone. "Daddy, I want to come home." She begins to cry. "I'm scared. Where is mommy?"

A sharp pain hits his forehead as his heart aches for his daughter. "Honey, don't be afraid. You know that me and your mother love you dearly." He pictures his wife's face. Water is building up in his eyes. "Hope.... I mean... "He pictures his wife being tortured by the mafia. "Wait, Tyra. I need you to listen to me." He moves the phone from his ear as he takes a deep breath. "Don't you ever forget how much me and your mother love you and Trevon." A flash of anger is apparent in his eyes. "Even... in our absence, I want you to know that we are always there with you." The pain returns. "As long... as long... as we as a family love one another, we are always together."

She stops crying. "Daddy, you sound sad."

He laughs as he tries to tuck away the pain. "No baby, I'm just a little sick. I have a cold."

"Okay, Daddy. But are you going to come get us as soon as you feel better?" she asks.

"Yes, dear. I will come get you as soon as I can," Rell says.

"Is mommy sick too?" Tyra asks.

"Yeah, but she'll feel better soon once she knows that you're feeling better and not scared anymore." Rell tries to reassure his little girl that everything is going to be alright.

"Okay daddy, I am not going to be scared anymore because I want you and mommy to let us come home soon." She covers the mouth piece as she whispers into it. "Daddy, I'm going to tell Trevon the same thing so that we can hurry and come home, okay?"

Smiling, Rell is feeling a tiny bit of relief. "Okay dear. Now let me speak with your brother before I hang up."

Trevon anxiously grabs the phone. "Hello, Daddy."

"Hey son, how are you doing?"

His little voice hesitates. "Daddy... I'm not... scared."

"That's good, son."

The child quickly retorts. "Now can I come home?"

He smiles at his son's determination. "Nah, not right now, but as soon as your mother and I get everything under control, we'll be down to pick up you and your sister."

The child begins to whimper. "But Daddy, I want to come home now."

The sound of his son's pain only hurts him more. However, this is not the time to mourn. It's time to fight back and stand strong.

He growls into the phone. "Trevon, I want you to listen to me." Lowering his voice, he finds that tone that lets his kids know he's serious about something. "There's nothing wrong with being afraid. Even the bravest of men are scared sometimes... But it is what you do after you realize how scared you are that determines whether you're a coward or a man." Clearing his throat, Rell tries to get the fear out of his voice. He's not just talking to his son; he's also talking to himself. "Listen to me. I want you to suck up those tears and take care of you and your sister until I come down to get you, alright?"

He sniffles, "Okay, Daddy."

Rell talks with Phillip's wife once more before ending the phone call. They make plans for their next phone call to be in a few hours.

As his friend leaves the apartment, Rell turns the TV back on and finds a news channel. He ponders deeply about what is happening to his wife and friends. He doesn't want to think about it, but he can't help it. Terrible thoughts keep popping in and out of his mind. He's ready to ask for another video.

He even forces himself to smile at the thought, but the problems continue to resurface.

It's been a while since his living nightmare began, and he has yet to watch the entire story on the news. Resting his elbows on his knees, Rell sits in front of the screen and turns up the volume.

A reporter comes on; she's in Brooklyn. She's saying a body has been found in the East River.

Rell sighs. "What's new?"

The woman continues by describing that the unidentified man was murdered execution style.

Rell changes the channel to find any news about his situation. Finally, after searching a hundred channels, he finds a station that's covering the story.

The news anchorman sits behind his large news desk as he describes how the law enforcement has yet to catch the cop killer. He gives a colorful explanation to how and why Rell could lose his mind and kill a hard-working detective of the New Jersey police department. The anchorman says that the reason for Marten O'Brien's body smelling like liquor on the night he died was due to the murderer being drunk as a skunk.

Rell falls back. He can't believe that they would paint not just a horrible story, but one with such an evil picture of lies.

The reporter moves on and displays Marten's photo on the screen. It's the first time that Rell has ever gotten a good look at his face.

Detective O'Brien is in full uniform. He looks like he was receiving a medal of honor at the time of when the picture was taken. It's before he went gray, or either he dyed it for the ceremony. His face seems fuller. His eyebrows aren't as thick as they were on the night of the incident. He doesn't appear to be as menacing as he did the night of the shooting. The picture has so many details. Rell can't stop comparing everything with the night that O'Brien was killed.

Rell's jaw drops. Suddenly, O'Brien looks so familiar. Rell's seen him somewhere before that night... but, where? He tries to think.

Supreme bursts in the apartment's front door. "Phillip is dead!"

Rell's insides feel like they just fell out. "Huh?"

Taking the remote control from his hand, Supreme tries to find the station. "It's on the news." Turning the channel once more, Supreme finally finds the story. "Here, on this channel."

The female is pointing to a body bag on the ground. "Yes, he's been identified by his driver's license. His name is Phillip Jenkins. His body was found floating in the East River this morning." She pushes her ear piece deeper into her ear as she ends her coverage. "Back to you, Jen."

At the station, the anchor announces the update on Marten O'Brien's strange wife. They begin by showing footage of her exiting the funeral.

Rell is beginning to panic. "Them bastards killed him!" He jumps up, still staring at the screen. "Those bastards killed Phillip! Those mafia bastards' killed him!"

Supreme grabs him and sits him back down. "Look. I need you to calm down and get yourself together. You just sit and get your thoughts together."

Lowering his voice, Rell feels so lost. "There's no need."

"What do you mean. . . there's no need?" Supreme asks.

"I know who the cop is now," Rell says.

"You know who he is?" Supreme asks.

"Yes, but first, I want to get those bastards who killed my friend, and then I'll get out of this country. . . with my wife and kids." His eyes turn into a vacuum of darkness. "For everything that I've always had to live for. . . I now, have that much more to die for."

Chapter Fourteen

Two park security guards are patrolling Jersey City's Liberty State Park. Matt McMillon and Jerris Chapman pull off of Morris Pesin Drive and park in a dimly lit corner of the parking lot near the picnic area.

McMillon pulls a cold can of beer from a six pack. "Here you go, bro."

"You see. There you go with that bro-stuff." Jerris snatches the can. "Why do all of you white people always call us black people, bro?" he asks.

"C'mon. Stop playing and relax your mind." Matt pops his can open. "It's bad enough that we have to be out here working the midnight shift, and I don't want to hear your so-called 'philosophical' bullshit tonight."

Jerris laughs at him. "Yo, You're lucky you're my friend, because if you weren't, I would have a problem with you calling my words   so-called 'philosophical'." He smiles. "I'm just playing with you, partner. This double shift is driving me crazy, too."

Holding his beer can up, Matt proposes a toast. "Don't worry bro. We're just going to sit here and get drunk tonight." They tap their cans together as they watch a car drive past. "You see that car? We're not even going to tell them the park is closed."

The car goes all the way to the picnic area and stops. The driver and the passenger get out first, and then go to the back door on the driver's side.

The two security guards are watching as they drink their beers.

"Hey bro, what type of car is that?" asks Matt.

"I don't know. I didn't give it a good look."

"You see. I know you wouldn't know what kind of car it was. You don't know your cars." McMillon and Chapman are staring at the suspicious car. Something definitely seems odd about the way the men are standing beside the car.

As the two men stand by the back door, it opens and another man steps out. All three of them begin to talk with each other.

"Hold up, partner. I know you think I don't know cars, but you're wrong. I just don't know many American cars." Taking another sip from his can, Jerris begins to brag. "Are you forgetting that I drive a BMW?"

"You see, bro – that's the problem. You're sending all of your money to another country, but you get upset about the lack of good jobs in our country," Matt states.

McMillon and Chapman begin to argue as the three men remain by the back door of the unknown car. After checking the area, one man leans into the back seat and pulls a half conscience woman to her feet. He leans her against his shoulder as one of the other men grab her other arm and drape it across their own shoulder.

Pointing at the car, Mac argues with his shift partner. "I'm telling you, Jerris! It's a goddamn Chevy!"

"Hold up partner," Jerris says. He takes a better look. ". Wait a sec. What are they doing with that guy?"

McMillon tries to think of a plausible explanation. "It looks like he's drunk, and they're just trying to get him to walk it off."

Chapman notices something. "Wait a minute. That's not a man. Look at her ass."

"Yeah, you're right, but what difference does it make?" Mac asks.

The three men take her down to the Liberty Walkway, right on the edge of the Hudson River. Her body is slumped. Only her head bobs up and down as they practically carry her on their shoulders.

The two security guards are quiet. They both had set their cans down a long time ago. They even opened the car's windows.

The woman holds her head up and begins to mumble. It drops again. Her feet are dragging on the pavement. One of her shoes comes off.

Giving his partner the eye, Jerris just can't believe what is happening. "You see that, partner?"

"Yeah, I seen it bro, and I think we need to check into this." Matt starts to think they won't be doing much drinking tonight.

It doesn't take long before the three men stop with the woman. One of the men climbs over the railing and stands on the rocks by the river. The other two men pick the lady up and pass her over to him. Then, one of them climbs over the railing to help the first man take the woman down to the edge of the river.

The two security guards are now out of their car and moving briskly.

The cold water hits the woman's flesh. She screams at the top of her lungs.

Both of the park officers yell out. "What the hell are you guys doing?"

The man that didn't climb over the rail, draws his gun and starts shooting at the unarmed security guards. His two partners begin to beat the woman with their fists.

The rent-a-cops run back to their car and radio in to their command.

Down by the edge of the river, one of the men picks up a boulder-sized rock and smashes it into the back of the woman's skull. The man spits her blood from his lips as her body collapses under water.

Back at their car, the park guards are scrambling to start the engine. "C'mon bro, give me the keys!" Jerris passes them to him, but they fall through his fingers. "Ah shit! They're on the floor!" They're both in pure panic mode.

The three thugs are running back towards the guard's car.

"Oh shit! Matt, they're coming!" More than anything, Jerris just wants the car to start.

Matt grabs the keys from the floor and sticks them in the ignition. The two are trying to keep their heads down as bullets are literally tearing their car apart. Glass is falling all around them. Holes are appearing out of nowhere. Finally, the car starts.

They drive off just as the gunmen make it off the walkway. The gunmen are cursing as they climb back into their car.

Across the river in a whole different world, Rell is sleeping like a champ. He's snoring like he hasn't slept in twenty years. He has the remote control clasped in his hand, and his arms are wrapped around his chest. For the first time since all of this has happened, he's able to sleep.

A loud thump is suddenly heard on the door. Again and again, the pounding continues.

Jumping to his feet, Rell is frantic. He thinks to himself. "This is the end. They got me. I have no way of getting out of here."

This time, the knock is accompanied by an old man's raspy voice. "Hey fool, open the door!"

Rell wrinkles his face in confusion and mumbles at the door. "Who is it?"

Hitting the door one more time, the man hollers at Rell. "It's ole man, fool! Open the door!"

Yanking the door open while reading his watch, Rell goes on. "Do you realize it's twelve-thirty in the middle of the night?" Rell looks him over from head to toe. "And who thuh hell are you?"

The old man looks to be sixty something. He has a salty white-colored afro. He's wearing a tight, bright yellow, polyester two-piece suit. The bellbottoms are hanging over his six inched stacked shoes. He resembles someone who's just stepped out of some type of time machine from the late seventies or the early eighties.

The old man looks around Rell. "I'm Supreme's grandfather.   Where are those two pretty girls?"

Rell steps into his view. "They're not here. Can you come back tomorrow?"

"Come back tomorrow? Boy, are you crazy?" Supreme's grandfather surveys the place again. "Well, just let me come on in and watch some TV."

Holding his position, Rell remains focused. "Sir, I don't even know your name. . ."

The old man cuts him off. "My name is Ole Man."

Rell pauses as he realizes why his longtime partner gave him this particular place. He even smirks at the thought of how slick his friend is.

"Well, Ole Man, it's almost one o'clock in the morning and I'm trying to sleep. Could you please come back later in the day?"

The grandpa whispers, "C'mon sonny, you have those two girlies in there with you, don't you?"

He laughs. "Sir, knowing that you're Supreme's grandfather, I can't lie to you – the women are not here with me."

Ole Man chuckles, and then persists on staying. "Well, let me see some TV then?"

Rell is becoming agitated and wants to go back to sleep. "Sir, no. You may not come in and watch television. However, you can come back at another time. I'm trying to sleep."

He mumbles, "Young punk."

"What did you call me?" Rell asks.

The grandfather repeats himself loud and clear. "I called you a punk, Fool. A punk."

"Alright, that's enough Ole Man. It's time for you to go." Rell is getting agitated.

He tries to close the door, but the old man steps in the path of the door. "C'mon, Ole Man, I'm trying to sleep."

"Well, fight me for it then, and the winner gets what they want." he says.

Rell sighs. "Fight you? Man, you're too old to fight. I don't want to fight you."

The Ole Man gives him a different option. "Okay, then we'll have a punch-out. We can punch each other until one of us gives up. Whoever gives up first, is the loser."

Rell stares at him for a second. He really would love to knock his old ass out but knows it's not a smart move. "Nah, Ole Man, I can't do that to you."

The rough old man gets loud. "Just like I thought, you're a young punk."

They bicker back and forth until Rell can't take anymore. "Alright, you old bastard. Looks like we're gonna do this your way, and I'll even give you the first hit." Holding his chin forward, Rell taunts him. "Hit me you old fool."

Ole Man jumps into his boxing stance and punches him with a good right jab.

Rell stumbles back. He has to admit the old man can hit pretty hard, but no knockout.

Rell raises his hands. "Alright, you old bastard. . . pucker up."

Ole man walks away laughing. "Shit, I just wanted to see if your dumb ass was stupid enough to stand here and let me hit your punk ass in the mouth." Waving goodbye, the old man bids his farewell. "Tell Preme, I checked on you." He's still laughing as he walks out of sight.

Checking his chin, Rell tastes the blood in his mouth. "Ole Man, you really need to get your slick ass back over to your place." Rell is furious now.

Rell slams the door behind him and goes back over to the couch. Now, he knows it will be awhile before he can fall back to sleep...not just because of his many problems, but now also because of his sore jaw.

Pressing the power button on the remote, he searches for something on television. A call comes in on the pre-paid cell. Remembering that Wanda, Phillip's wife, had agreed to call him the following morning, he knows it couldn't be her on the other end -unless it is an emergency. Picking up the phone, he hopes it's the same person that he's been texting all night. There's no time for any more mistakes, and he has to get to the bottom of this.

Viewing the screen first, he doesn't recognize the number. Pressing send, he remembers to disguise his voice like someone who woken up by a phone ringing. Clearing his throat, he answers. "Hmm, hello." It must be the person he was hoping for, because he quickly converts back to his normal voice. "Wait, don't hang up. It's me. I just wanted to make sure it was you." Standing to his feet, he interrupts the caller. "Wait, don't say anything else on the phone. We have to talk face to face. Things are too crazy right now. So please, don't say anything on the phone. I'll be able to hear everything you have to say when we meet." Rubbing his forehead, he repeats the caller's words. "Where?"

He paces the floor a couple times. "I got it. . . do you remember the last place we met?" It takes a couple seconds for the caller to remember. "Yes, that's it, but don't say the name on the phone. I'll have someone pick you up there later today." He ends the call.

Detective Stephens and Price come on to the Liberty State Park scene. They're surprised by the fact that there are only two patrol cars in the parking lot.

Detective Stephens' big frame climbs out of the car. "Who's in charge out here?" he asks.

A young officer walks up. "I am, sir."

Stephens points at the young fellow. "You?"

"Yessir..." he says.

"No, you're not. From this point on, I'm in charge." Stephens walks past him. "Where are the witnesses?" he asks.

The young officer catches up to him. "Sir, I was told that Detective Boyle was in route, and he didn't want anyone to disturb anything until he got here."

Stephens stops and inspects the officer from head to toe. "Let me tell you something, you fucking moron. This is my district, and I'll do my job...". He searches for the eyes of the remaining officers in the parking lot. "...In my goddamn district until this stupid ass Doyle or Boyle can have my captain tell me different." His partner, Price, is walking in his direction. "Price, please get this dumb ass rookie out of my fucking face before I drop him. I swear to God, I'm not in the mood." Walking away he yells to anyone that can hear him. "And someone tell me where the fucking witnesses are before I shoot someone!"

As another cop rushes over to escort him, he adds one more item to his list of demands.

"Where's the body?" Obviously, Stephens is in no mood for games today.

"Sir, we couldn't find a body." The cop continues. "The two guys smelled like a pair of beer distilleries. We have reason to believe that they were just drunk and got into it with some young thugs."

The two security guards are sitting on the hood of their car. Its windshield has bullet holes and spider webbed patterns of cracked and broken glass all the way across. The side windows are completely gone, and the two front wheels are flat from hitting the curb.

Stephens inspects the pair as he slowly approaches them. In his twenty years of experience, he's pretty much seen every type of drunk and criminal possible. However, there's a problem. The two men don't look drunk.

He stops in front of them. The rookie was correct. The smell of beer hits him directly in the face. Stephens doesn't say a word. He watches them for a couple of seconds, and then he flashes his badge.

"Okay, let me get one thing straight. I heard on my radio that there was a female being murdered." His eyes bounce from one to the other. "I want you both to know that if you're playing with a woman's life, or simply wasting my time, you just royally fucked up." Drawing a pack of gum from his pocket, he pauses his thought He opens the silver wrapper as he finishes his words. "Where is the woman?"

The black guard, the one called 'bro' by his partner, interjects and points to the walkway. "Man, we already told them that she was down there, but the cops didn't even go all the way down to the water.

"They didn't?" Stephens looks to the officer who had just escorted him over.

The officer quickly tries to cover his ass. "Sir, I followed all orders."

"Hmm. . ." Stephens turns back to his witnesses. "Okay, you show me where all of this happened." The two men jump from the hood of their car and head toward the walkway.

As he walks down to the edge of the Hudson River, Stephens hopes like any other good officer of the law that there is no dead body. It's been a long night, and he doesn't want to be played with by two drunks. However, he'd rather deal with that than - have to handle an additional homicide this week.

Price catches up to his partner. They both see quite a few bullet shells scattered across the pavement as they enter the walkway. Price sticks a piece of red tape beside some of the shells.

The security guards run forward. "There she is!" They see her body. "Here she is!" Jerris climbs over the rail. "Here she is!" he says, even louder than before.

Stephens and his partner simultaneously yell out to the guards. "Don't touch her!"

Price draws his radio from his left hip and radios in to the station. Stephens sprints to the guard's location, hopping the rail like it was branch on the ground.

Price stumbles on a rock as he gets closer to the woman's position. Again, he says, "Back away from her!" He kneels down beside her and checks her vital signs. "Get an ambulance out here!" He can't believe it, but he feels a faint pulse. "She's alive! She's alive!" He looks at the security guards. "Take your coats off and go get some blankets! Quick!"

Her body is face down. Her clothes are soaked in blood. Her entire head is swollen like a balloon. It's a purplish color with red streaks of blood lining her face in a parallel pattern.

The white guard, McMillon, jumps into the river and within seconds holds something up. "Here's her purse!" he yells.

Stephens doesn't even turn back to look. "Check the inside of it for her name." He calls out to Chapman next. "You! Get down here and help me carry her up."

He doesn't want to disturb the crime scene, but she needs to be moved to a dryer area. The two men grab her petite frame, carefully and slowly carrying her back up the small slope of rocks. Price and a few more officers meet them at the other side of the railing. One of the rookies wraps her body with a blanket as they move her to a nearby picnic table.

Stephens yells out a reminder before they lay her down. "Don't lay her flat! Keep her head elevated!"

Before Stephens can get to her, an ambulance pulls up. It must have been in the area. Stephens is really pissed; he can't stand to see anyone do something to a woman. It's not only women, though. It's any person, really. However, women are very dear to him because his mother was murdered when he was only ten years old.

The detective moving toward the ambulance like a man on fire. The paramedics are checking her vital signs and disrobing her body of her wet clothes.

McMillon, the guard who found the purse, is running up behind him. "Her name is Sheila Jacobs!" he says as he catches up with Stephens. McMillon's out of breath. His face is red and sweaty. "Her name. . ." Taking another breath, he tries again. "Her name. . . is. . .."

He can't get it out, so he passes the driver's license to the detective. Stephens glances at it. He does a double take, and then pauses. He calls his partner over. They both check out her identification, and then turn to get a better look at her.

Stephens summons the ambulance driver over. "Listen, I want you to make sure that she makes it to the hospital." The driver attempts to say something, but the detective holds his index finger up for him to hold his words. "My partner, Detective Price, is going to escort you. I don't want you to stop until you get to that hospital. You understand?" The driver nods his head as he faces the two park guards. "You two – I don't want you guys to talk to anyone other than me. I don't care if they're holding a gun to your fucking head – you talk to no one. Understand? If I find out you've talked, I'll lock the two of you up for drinking in public and I'll personally make sure that you lose your jobs."

After the ambulance drives away, Stephens checks the woman's ID again. Everyone on the force knows the name of a cop-killer's wife. He says her name under his breath.

Peering at the Hudson River, he mumbles the million dollar question. "Sheila Jacobs, what just happen?"

Chapter Fifteen

There's a meeting being held at the Internal Affairs Office. It was called by the detective team of Joseph Brown and Tom Riley. The colleagues are reviewing the video over and over while having a think-tank session.

They are viewing the scene where Rell and Martin O'Brien are tussling only a few feet away from the hood of the patrol car. The sound of the gun goes off, once. And then it goes off again. The two men stop fighting and stand to their feet. Their faces show zero expression; the blankness is visibly seen by the detectives. Suddenly, the weakness hits Martin O'Brien. His hand clamps to the hood of his patrol car as his frame slumps over. His legs buckle, and he falls back to his death.

Tom pauses the video as soon as the gun fire starts penetrating the wind shield. "You guys see that?" he asks, pointing Rell's face out to the three other invited detectives. "Why would a banker with a promising future destroy his life by killing an officer of the law?" Looking to the one female and the other two men in the room, he continues. "His name is Terrell Jacobs!" He pokes the screen. "A Banker! He's not some thug! He's a goddamn banker! So, why? Why would he kill a cop?"

The thirty-something-looking black female IAD detective holds up her index finger and clears her throat.

Lowering his voice, Tom points to her. "Yes, Elizabeth."

First, she adjusts her glasses as she checks some of her notes. She grabs the remote control and rewinds the video to where the knife falls from Marten O'Brien's hand.

Freezing the frame, she poses her question. "Why did O'Brien have a knife? He had a gun."
The video forensic team did a great job. Everything is crystal clear. Even in the present scene at a half of a block distance away, all figures can be clearly seen, with the exception of their faces. However, it's still very obvious who the two main subjects are.

Reflecting back to her pad, she reads another of her scribbles." I also need to know why we haven't identified the other three suspects."

Big Joe interrupts. "Two of the suspects are believed to be Reyquan Lewis and Carlos Martinez."

"Okay, so where's the other one? And, have you questioned the two suspects that you just named?"

Big Joe points to a folder positioned in front of her. "Check your folder. They're both deceased. They died in the accused murderer's car. It seems they died in a wreck while trying to flee the crime scene."

Tom cuts in. "Listen, I know it's early and we asked you guys at the last moment to assist us on the case, but it's important that we find out exactly what's going on. I'm pretty sure that after you guys saw the video, you want to know what in the hell is going on, too." He snatches his pen from his pocket and slams it against the wall. "I think that bastard Brewkowski's hiding something that can save this Terrell Jacobs' life!"

Elizabeth rewinds the video further back. "Here." Pointing to the scene where Martin O'Brien jumps from behind a group of bushes, she narrates for the men. "O'Brien attacked the first man. Had they been chasing O'Brien to make him attack like that? And if they were – why didn't O'Brien just use his gun?" She speeds the frame forward to where Rell intervened. "Right here. You see. After he tackled him, he waved his friends away." She pauses the frame again. "All right guys. I'm going to play this again, but in slow motion. I want to make sure that I see what I thought I saw the first time." She hits the play button, and continues to talk as the video slowly goes scene by scene. "You see there? He's telling his friend to move back. Look at how he's waving his arm back." Elizabeth holds her breath for a second. "Okay, here. Marten O'Brien is stabbing at him, but the suspect is still trying to talk with him. There, O'Brien stabs again and the suspect knocks the weapon from his hand." Slowing the frame even more, she wants to make sure she understands the events on the video. "Watch his head. He's looking down to O'Brien's waist. This is where the suspect tackles O'Brien." She turns to her colleagues. "Why now?" she asks them. She removes the slow-motion option and allows the video to play at its regular pace. "Why is it now that Ryan Brewkowski is finally coming to his partner's aid?" They all stare as the car's camera draws closer to the brawl and stops within inches of the two fighting. Elizabeth pauses the frame when O'Brien's hand lands on the hood of the car. "Was it Brewkoski's plan for his partner to die?" she wonders aloud.

Big Joe stands to his feet. "Okay Elizabeth, you've done great." He motions to a chair and waits for her to rest her back against the chair's stern frame before he starts talking again. "I stopped you because you guys have seen and figured out so much without knowing or having all of the information." He studies their frozen faces before going further. "Please, pull out your pens. I have some additional facts to give you, along with some interesting information." Their pens were already in their hands, but he just wanted the importance of the matter to sink into their minds.

The showing of the video served its true purpose. Big Joe and Tom had intended for their three invited guests to come to the same conclusion as their own, but they need more help on how to figure this puzzle out. And more importantly, they want to know why the Jersey City police force hasn't said or done anything about the flaws in the video.

Pulling out a sheet of paper, Big Joe reads from it. "First fact, and one that's very important, is that Debbie O'Brien had a 400,000-dollar insurance policy on her husband. At the funeral, she seemed like she didn't give a damn about his death. She wouldn't even ride in the hearse with any of the family, let alone by herself. She drove her own car, and she wouldn't even dress in black. The last time that anyone saw her was at the funeral before a strange man gave her an interesting envelope. Its contents are unknown to us at this time."

Tom stands to his feet and takes over for his partner. "Before she left the funeral, however... she seemed to have a confused romantic moment with Detective Brewkowski..." He allows his words to linger in the air for a moment before moving onward. "Marten O'Brien's alcohol level was pretty high. He was drunk on the night of his murder. In fact, there are rumors that Brewkowski was also drunk on that same night, but we can't find any evidence to prove it." He stops and gives the three detectives time to jot down their notes. "When we interrogated Detective Brewkowski. . ." His listeners raise their heads. "Yes." Riley nods his head in confirmation. "We did have the opportunity to speak with him, but as soon as we started asking questions, he requested that his lawyer be present. He seemed very nervous and agitated when he left."

Standing to his feet, Big Joe waves his hand to get his partner's attention. "Don't forget the B and E story," he says.

Winking his eye at his big friend, Tom continues. "Yes, that is another story that Brewkowski told us. He said that they were there to do a sting for a local robbery... But guess what? We checked all records and there is not now, nor was there then, any problem with breaking and entering crimes."

The meeting room's phone begins to ring. Someone knocks on the door at the same time. Joe opens the door, and Tom answers the phone.

A short, stout man with a bad tan is standing at the door. He's wearing a cheap, wrinkled suit with ketchup stains on his tie. He seems to be very nervous in the presence of Big Joe. Even his palms are sweaty and clammy.

He passes the big guy a sheet of paper with an address written on it. "We just found out that Terrell Jacob's wife was found this morning- half dead. She's at the hospital now, and captain wants you guys to go and check her out."

Tom receives the same information on the phone. He and his partner stop everything. Even their heart rates momentarily slow down to process the new information. They grab their coats as they run out the door.

Chapter Sixteen

The sun rays are beaming through to the couch where Rell sits. He's been up all morning. He's unable to get his children and wife off of his mind.

He reflects to the good times, a few years back. Sheila was happy. He was happy and so were the children. It was early in the morning when Tyra and Trevon climbed into bed with their parents. He smiled because the kids caught them kissing that day. Trevon had asked him why he had his tongue in mommy's mouth. He even asked if he was trying to choke mommy with his tongue.

Sheila hugged Tyra tight in her arms and asked her what was her greatest wish. The child told her mother that she wanted her mother and daddy to always love each other like they do now. Rell and his wife kissed and promised that her wish was granted.

Trevon hopped up and declared that he had a wish, too. Rell and Sheila faced him and asked to hear his wish. Trevon blushed and said that he wishes to grow up and be just like his father.

His blood red eyes squeeze what little water they can manage from his eye sockets. His head is throbbing with a major headache. The thoughts of his once perfect marriage keep popping in and out of his mind. "What happened. How could their once perfect love turn into the misery that they had begun to live in prior to the mess.... And this mess, how did it all come to this?" Reyquan and Carlos are dead. Phillip's body has been found in the river. Sheila has been snatched by the mafia, and he's been imprisoned inside of this estranged apartment, not knowing what to do or how to do it.

Supreme walks in and startles his friend. "Yo! What's up?"

Stopping in his tracks, he sees the look on Rell's face. "My bad, I didn't mean to scare you, Rell."

Falling back on the couch, he rubs the faint tears from his face. "Whoa." Rell takes a deep sigh. "You're cool man. I'm all right."

Holding his position, Supreme is direct with him. "Man, you don't look all right. You look like you haven't slept in months."

"Well, I would have slept if you'd told me about that guy who says he's your grandfather, yet I've never heard you even mention him."

Cracking a smile, Supreme backs away to the kitchen. "Who? Ole Man?" Unable to hold back his laughter any longer, he chuckles out loud. "Yeah, he's my grandfather from my father's side. What happened last night?"

Rell repeats his story to his pal. "What happened?" Shaking his head, he thinks back to the night's events. "You should be asking what didn't happen. That bastard hit me in my mouth!"

Covering his mouth as he laughs, Supreme tries to catch a breath. "Wait a minute, you didn't fall for that old trick of his, did you?"

The shame is inked all over Rell's face. "Yeah, he got me that time. That ole bastard came here looking for your two lady friends last night. I wouldn't let him in, so he tricked me into letting him hit me in my mouth."

Supreme falls out on the floor with laughter. "You let my grandpops knock your ass out!"

His friend's actions are really pissing him off. He speaks sternly. "No... your grandfather didn't knock anyone out. He just swelled my jaw a little bit."

Supreme laughs even louder. "Shit, that's bad enough!"

Not smiling anymore, Rell waits for his good friend to stop laughing. "So have you found anything out from any of your mafia associates?"

The seriousness lands back on his face. "Nah, not yet, but I should know something very soon. You know how those Italians are – they keep pretty tight-lipped."

"I thought you said that you have some good Italian friends that would tell you where my wife is and who killed Phillip?"

"I do, but none of them have heard anything yet." Getting up from the floor, the glare on his face becomes as hard as concrete. "Let me explain something to you. I don't care if the president killed Phillip. He, too, would be run down and drug down the streets like a dog. No one is going to get away with this." Drawing the Berretta from the rear of his waist, he keeps going. "Don't you believe that shit you see in movies – that the mafia wants beef with any mutha fucka's from Brooklyn... I promise you, if they know who did this, they will pass him over to me before I destroy everything they love. Right now, my crew is riding through their neighborhoods and setting up at the same time. Believe me, they don't wanna fuck with a gangsta like me."

"All right, but I do have one another favor. I need you to go and pick someone up."

"Who?" Supreme asks.

"It's a person with some very important information. She'll be at the Hard Rock Café."

"Who is she?" Supreme wants to know who is so important.

"Preme, who she is, is irrelevant. I just need you to meet her at the rear of the building."

"How will I know who she is?" he asks.

Rell knows she'll find Supreme. "Don't worry, her sister works the door. When you get there, just ask for my special seat."

"Your seat?" Supreme's not sure if he even wants to know what 'special' means in this instance.

"Yes, Rell's special seat..." Rell grins like a Cheshire cat.

Chapter Seventeen

She's located deep within the Intensive Care Unit. Her room is brightly lit. Tubes and needles are penetrating everything from the back of her hands, to the veins of her wrist, and even her forearms. A catheter has been inserted into her urinary track. Tubes are coming out of her nose and mouth, and her body is barely alive. She's only surviving by a life support system.

Sheila has already been through several surgeries. The doctors have done everything they can do to save her life. Now, the rest is up to her and God.

Detective Stephens is the only one in her room. Due to the severity of the crime, only family is allowed to visit – and she has no family in Jersey. All of her family is in Georgia. They have been notified and hopefully will be coming to see her soon.

He sits in a lone chair by her bed. The detective is engulfed by all of the flowers that her coworkers and many friends have sent up to her room. He tries his best not to look at her beautiful face that's trapped within that tight bandage around her head. Besides that, he can't stand the look of the neck brace that she's in. It looks like it's choking the life right out of her. It's so painful for him to watch. All of this reminds him of how his mother was right before she died; she was barely hanging on, and the machines and tubes were everywhere. The picture never leaves his mind. Just sitting in his seat brings back so much unwanted pain.

While in his thoughts, he reflects back to the day his mother was murdered. He was only a boy. His mother had just walked him home from school when she saw the drunk married couple next door in an argument. The couple started fighting. Stephens' mother kept watching. The husband had just slammed his wife to the ground and was beating her like she was a grown man. Stephens' mother immediately ran over and pulled him off of his wife, begging them to stop fighting. In the blink of an eye, the husband had drawn his gun from out of nowhere and shot the Stephens' mother in her chest... twice.

Stephens' eyes are red with grief. The last words his mother said pop into his mind. " Dear child, when you grow up, don't let this happen to anyone else... I love you." He has never forgotten those words. Those words are reasons he does what he does, and why he takes his job so seriously.

There's a light tap on Sheila's hospital room door. Big Joe and Tom walk in and greet Detective Stephens.

Stretching his arm out to shake hands, the feisty Irish introduces himself first. "Hi, how are you doing? We're with the IAD. My name is Tom Riley, and my partner right here is Joseph Brown." They release hands. "Are you the guy who found her?"

"Yes, I'm Detective Stephens." He looks over to Sheila and back to the IAD pair. "I'm also the guy who notified your department that she was here."

His words catch their attention. They lean in. "Why", they both ask?

The two are surprised because it's not too often that a cop from the Jersey force would even think of calling their so-called "deadliest enemy". Maybe not all of them, but ninety-nine percent of the cops in every city across the nation hate their Internal Affairs Department.

Stephens doesn't even flinch. "I called you guys because nothing seemed right last night." He squeezes his thick meaty fingers into a massive fist. "The witnesses..."

The two cut him off. "You have witnesses?" Okay. So maybe now they're getting somewhere.

"Yes, and they are in a safe location until you guys can find them a safe house." Stephens says.

Tom repeats his words. "A safe house?" Now he is utterly confused.

"For what?" he says. "Why?"

Stephens fills them in on his theory. "I have reason to believe that the mafia was involved in last night's incident."

Big Joe pulls up a chair and sits. "Hmm, tell us more."

Detective Stephens relays everything the two security guards told him of the crime that they saw. He further emphasizes that all of the men were - white and seemed to be very calm at what they were doing.

Resting his chin on his thumb, Big Joe asks the pertinent question on his mind. "So why are you involving the IAD? It's only the mafia – you're on the police. You guys can handle that by yourself."

Stephens tries to explain. "You guys don't understand. I asked that you come here because last night, when I got to the location, every law officer on the scene was shocked that my partner and I were there. They weren't expecting us to show up. I had overheard the call on the radio so, we just showed up at the scene."

The big guy pulls out his pad, and Tom draws his out moments after. With pens and pads ready, they give Stephens the nod to go ahead and continue.

Stephen begins…"I can't really prove it, but it seemed like the officers who were on the scene when I arrived were just standing around, waiting for the victim to die".

Big Joe's jaw drops. "Why do you say that?" he asks the detective.

Detective Stephens explains his reasoning. "Her body was only a few yards from their parked cars and, according to the security guards that witnessed the woman's attack, the officers never even made an attempt to locate her body." He gives the two a couple of seconds to soak in the information and jot some notes. "The officers claimed their reason for not thoroughly searching was because the two security guards seemed intoxicated, although it was very evident that they weren't drunk at all."

Big Joe asks, "What are the names of those officers who were at the scene?"

Pulling a sheet of paper from his shirt pocket, Stephens grins. "I wrote all of them down." He passes over the list. "Here, you can have it."

Riley and Brown read over the names. They're hoping that something might stand out;

they might recognize some, or at least one, of the names. Someone that they've investigated before would be an added bonus.

Stephens looks over to Sheila's bed. He begins to speak to no one in particular. "The doctor said that she has a slim chance of making it. When he examined her, he found that they forced liquor down her throat to get her drunk. She also had ecstasy and cocaine in her system." Standing to his feet, Stephens walks over to her body and pats her shoulder. "Her brain is swollen, and her spine is fractured in three places, including her neck." One of the monitors begins to beep. "We're lucky, she didn't die from hypothermia. She barely had a pulse when I got to her."

A nurse interrupts his thoughts by rushing into the room. She immediately checks the beeping monitor. After she's satisfied the alarm was for what she thought it was for, she presses the button to cancel and silent the alarm. She then unhooks the empty clear pouch hanging next to Sheila's bed, and replaces the empty hook with a new bag of the necessary clear liquid medication.

Stephens waits until the nurse closes the door upon leaving. "The witnesses, stated that she started screaming when she was near the water."

Tom blurts, "The cold water must have startled her."

Stephens nods his head. "And that's when they beat her. . ."

Softly rubbing her arm, Stephens tries to somewhat gather his composure. "Those bastards beat her with one of those large rocks down by the river and crushed her skull in. . . . which is why her brain is swollen."

Big Joe keeps his eyes glued to his pad. "All right, I need you to be specific. How do you know that the perps were affiliated with the mafia? And, more importantly, what mafia group do you suspect?"

Stephens answers as specific as he can. "Well, my witnesses think the suspects were of Italian decent. I questioned the security guards separately and they both said that they could clearly hear Italian accents as the suspects yelled at them as they were firing their weapons." He pauses. "Ah, Detective Riley, I believe your phone is vibrating."

Grabbing his phone, Riley feels slightly embarrassed. "I apologize. It's the office." He only talks on it for a few seconds before he ends the call. Riley focuses back to his conversation with Stephens. "Okay, something very important has popped up. We need the location of your witnesses and we'll be having some men sent here to assist you with the watching over her."

Stephens writes something on a piece of paper and passes it to the IAD team. "My partner, Price, will be there. He already knows that you should be coming, but please call and let him know when you guys are in the area – he's a little edgy these days."

Big Joe follows behind his partner as Tom rushes for the elevator. Joe doesn't even give the doors a chance to close before he begins to ask questions. Tom enjoys the thought of savoring the surprise for the ride in the car, but his big partner isn't about to let that happen.

The big guy presses the emergency stop button. "All right, what's going on?"

Tom can't hold it back. "We have one of New Jersey's finest at our station, and he's ready to talk. The captain wants us down there now."

Chapter Eighteen

The two IAD detectives race across town in less than thirty minutes. Their tires make a screeching sound as they slam their breaks, turning into the department's parking lot. Stopping their car at the building entrance- forget parking- they fling the doors wide open, jump from their seats, and race inside. The keys are still hanging from the car's ignition.

They hop of the elevator on the third floor, wasting no time on their usual friendly greetings to their co-workers. Their anticipation is at an all-time high. Each wondering what does this officer of law have to tell them? Could he have some information about the possible affair between Detective Brewkowski and O'Brien's wife? Could it be about a mafia connection between the department and O'Brien's death?

The pair do their best to keep open minds as they approach the interrogation room at the rear of the building. Instead of entering the room where the officer is waiting, they enter the room next door.

Their captain is already standing in the observation room, glaring through the transparent mirror with his arms folded across his chest. Keeping his arms tight against him, he begins to rub his square chin while in deep thought before turning and noticing his subordinates entering from behind.

All three stand within a foot of the glass. There's complete silence. Each one doing his best to evaluate the subject before they begin questioning him.

The nervous officer is sitting behind an old, gray government table. He's fumbling with his fingers. His young- looks to be in his early twenties. His short blond hair is a total mess. He obviously couldn't get any sleep last night. On one side of his head, the hair is flat against his skull. On the other, it's frizzy and tangled. He looks like he fell asleep drunk last night.

Even his uniform is a wreck. It looks like he grabbed it from a trash can prior to leaving his place.

His skin is a pale yellowish hue. He seems to have been vomiting all morning which is probably why he's slouched in the seat – then again, it could be that he's overwhelmed with problems.

The captain mumbles, "His father was a great officer."

Without moving his eyes, Big Joe asks, "Who was his father?"

"Is. . . not was. He's retired, and his name is William O'Miley."

"You mean the great Lieutenant O'Miley?" Big Joe asks in awe.

"Yes. . ." Cutting his eyes to his face, "That's who."

The captain's affirmative "yes" freezes into Big Joe's and Tom's minds. They quickly glance to each other in amazement.

The young officer's father, Lieutenant O'Miley, is a New Jersey police department decorated hero. He's one of the most recognized officers to go through the department.

He's done many things: from working to crumble the Italian mob, to saving his fellow

185

officer's lives during duty, to using most of his free time to save young children from the crime infested inner city streets.

The clock was already moving fast. However, now that they've realized who they have in their interrogation room, time has just sped up even faster. It won't be long before the disheveled officer's father has some fancy lawyer sent to the IAD, asking that the questioning stop.

Big Joe speaks smooth, but swift. Looking to the captain, he tries to gather any missed information. "Sir, what has he said, so far?"

Shaking his head, the captain sighed. "Nothing, really. He only said that he had some information for you guys, and he didn't want to speak to anyone else."

The two-man team walks into the small interrogation room. Big Joe's body language is stern and stiff. His partner is wearing a forced smile on the center of his face. Grabbing a chair, Big Joe twists it around and sits with his arms folded across the back rest.

The Irish detective walks around to the boyish looking rookie and places a hand on his shoulder. "You doing okay, son?"

Nodding his head with dread, the rookie's expression doesn't match. "Yeah, I guess. I'm as good as it gets nowadays."

Riley walks around O'Miley and takes a seat next to his partner. "So why is it that you want to speak with us?" Riley asks.

"I heard that you two are handling Detective O'Brien's case," the young cop says.

Leaning back in his chair, Riley folds his arms against his chest. "Okay, we are. Now, what does that mean to you?"

O'Miley's blood-red eyes spell nothing but fear and confusion. Rubbing the sweat from his face with his clammy palm, he tries to answer. "It... it." He rubs a tear from his cheek. "It means that I want to make a deal for the information that I have."

Big Joe presses his arms against the chair. "Wait, how do we know that you have good enough information for a deal? And why would you need a deal for our case?"

His voice cracks as he struggles to speak through his dry, clammy throat. "I... I know of some murders that were committed by officers of the law." He looks at the two before dropping his head back down. "I know the entire details about Officer O'Brien's murder, and I can confirm Terrell Jacob's innocence." The room goes silent as the information is being absorbed.

Tom and Big Joe look at one another. "Innocent?" they shout.

Officer O'Miley only lifts his head for a brief second. "Yes, he's innocent, but he may die if we don't hurry and save his life."

Someone knocks on the door.

Big Joe stands from his chair, opens the door, and steps out into the hallway. In less than five minutes, he returns.

Closing the door, Big Joe keeps his hand on the handle and just stands there. "I just talked with an FBI agent that says we have a deal if you can give us some incriminating evidence against these rogue officers." Joe reaches in his pocket to grab one of his peppermint candies before finishing the deal terms. "And we must be able to get a conviction with you as a witness. Are you ready to go all the way?"

Nodding his head, the O'Miley agrees. "Yes, I'm ready. May I have a glass of water?"

Unraveling the candy packet, Big Joe throws the piece into his mouth. "Yes, I'll have someone bring you a glass." He turns to the two-way mirror and nods his head for someone to bring the water. "Now, give me what I need to know, so that we can get these rogue bastards off the streets and out of uniform." Big Joe hopes none of his friends are involved but will nail their asses just the same if they are crossing the line.

"What do you want to know about first?" O'Miley asks.

"Tell us about murders," Joe says.

"Reyquan Lewis and Carlos Martinez..." He stares the two detectives down slowly and continues his story. "Those two were the first that I found out about. They were murdered in cold blood. Do you know, who they were?"

The two detectives have been working too hard on this case to not recognize those two mentioned names. However, they don't want to take the lead from their informant.

Joe turns to his partner and gives him the opportunity to respond.

Tom shakes his head as he stares back to his big partner. "Nah, we don't." Leaning in closer to their informant, Tom keeps up the charade. "Who were they?" he asks. The detectives pretend like they know absolutely nothing. They want to hear O'Miley's version of all that's happened.

Their snitch begins to speak, but he quickly stops once the door is knocked on.

The big detective, Joseph Brown, hops up and opens the door. Someone passes him an empty glass and a pitcher of ice water.

His large frame turns around and walks back to O'Miley. "Here's your water." Setting the items on the little table, he reaches for something else. "We also have some chilled soda, too, if you would like that instead."

O'Miley grabs the pitcher of water. "No, thank you. I prefer some water, right now." Suddenly, he goes into a mental trance. It's like he's back at the first scene of a crime. "I was in the car with my partner that night. He'd just gotten off of his cell phone. He looked pale after he hung up the phone. I asked him what's wrong. I mean, like did something happen to his wife or children or something." Taking a gulp of water from his glass, he proceeds with the night. "At first, my partner wouldn't say a word. And then, he asked me to be on the lookout for a silver LS 500 Lexus." O'Miley stops and looks at the detectives.

The two IAD partners are taking many notes as he continues.

"We pulled over to the curve and waited. And then out of nowhere, the Lexus zoomed past. That's when it all happened...". O'Miley stares off into the corner of the room.

Tom and his partner lean forward. "What Happened? What?" Tom asks.

"We took off in pursuit. He started telling me to be calm and not to panic." O'Miley holds his palms up. "I didn't know why he was telling me to be calm, but I just followed his lead anyway," he says.

O'Miley takes another sip from his glass. "We weren't in a marked car, so they didn't recognize us immediately. We pulled right beside them, and that's when my partner drew his weapon and shot a round right at them. I think he was trying to miss, because it was an easy shot, even while driving. We were right beside them."

Detective Riley stops him. "Why were you guys shooting at him?" he asks.

"Not us-- him... And I didn't know why at the time, but he scared them, and they took off. We were going almost a hundred when my partner side swiped their tail end. They lost control and rammed that pole. Their car was totaled. I just knew that no one could've lived through that, but they were alive." The young cop's face is pitiful.

The two partners stare at him. "Okay, what happened?"

"We backed up our patrol car to their position, and I jumped out to check on them. My partner got to them after me, but... "O'Miley stops talking and starts quietly sobbing.

The two partners say nothing. They just wait for him to regain control of himself.

Tears still swell in the corners of the rookie's eye sockets. The veins in his forehead start to bulge. He begins to shake his head like a wild man. "I didn't know he was going to kill them. I didn't know." Dropping his face into the darkness of his palms, O'Miley completely breaks down.

Joe hits the table. "What happened? Tell me, dammit!"

Their informant yells against the palms of his hands like a mad man. "He killed them!"

"How?... Boy, you better answer the fuckin' question!" Big Joe is fuming.

"He snapped their necks!" His eyes jump from side to side like a ping pong ball in a vicious tournament "The two were in a daze after the collision with the street light. My partner just went from one to another and snapped their necks. Just like that." His breathing quickens even faster. "He killed them both in cold blood." O'Miley is in shock.

Big Joe makes a note for their bodies to be re-examined. "Was it someone on the inside who examined them?" Joe asks.

O'Miley nods. "Yes. I was told that it was someone close, someone tied in with them."

"Them?" Tom asks.

"Yes, there's a lot of them." O'Miley can't believe he's being a rat, but he cannot live with this information anymore. It's literally eating him from the inside out. Uniforms are supposed to serve and protect, not take and harm.

The big guy stands up. "Them who?"

"The Irish blood," O'Miley replies.

Chapter Nineteen

Rell has been awake all morning, and all morning he's been pacing the living room floor. He's so confused and stressed; he doesn't know what to do. The world seems to have collapsed on his shoulders.

Even though he and Sheila were on the verge of a serious divorce, he would never wish any harm on her. He still loves her today like he did the day that he had seen the depth of her beautiful heart. He doesn't understand what destroyed their relationship, but he knows it's been over between the two of them for a long time.

His head begins to ache again. His eyes fill up like a flooded river. He can only imagine what these terrible people might be doing to his children's mother. Only his worst nightmares flash across his thoughts. The worst part is that it's apparently all about a supposed job contract that his best friend had worked hard to get.

Now, Phillip is dead. All because these Italians were too greedy to let it all go. However, they all made a very serious mistake. They don't know that they did harm to a good man, who has very good friends who would've died in a split second to save him. The mafia has no idea what they just got themselves caught in. It's a web that even Spiderman can't get out of.

Rell's mind comes back to the present. There's someone placing a key into the door's lock. The door knob turns. The door suddenly swings open before Rell has a chance to even consider a move. It's Supreme.

Rell is relieved to see his friend. "Where is she? Did you find her?" Rell asks.

Shaking his head, Supreme appears a bit frustrated. "What? Did I find her?" Walking in the apartment, he keeps on. "Did I find her? Man, you and that woman had me driving all over this city looking for her." Walking into the kitchen, Supreme opens a cabinet to grab a clean glass. "Man, you didn't tell me that you were going to have me out there for hours on end, searching for your people." Moving over to the sink, he rinses his glass and fills it with water. "I could have been doing more important---"

Rell cuts him off, only wanting a straight answer. "Supreme, tell me. Did you find her?"

Shaking his head, Supreme isn't going to play by Rell's rules. "Oh no, you're going to listen to me." He drinks half of the small glass of water. "I thought I only had to go to one place, but you tricked me into going to several places looking for this woman."

"Preme, did you find her? Rell asks again.

Supreme still doesn't answer. "What's so important about her? Does she know how much trouble you're in?"

Rell is getting very pissed off. "Preme, did you or didn't you find her?"

Supreme walks back over to the front door. "I had to make sure that everything was clear." Opening the front door, a slender woman with an ivory complexion walks in. "Yes, of course, I found her." Supreme flashes a big smile. "You seemed like you had lost faith in me."

The ivory lady is dressed like an extreme rock band groupie. Her hair is purple and black. Her eyeliner, lip stick, fingernails and toenails are solid black. She's wearing tight, black leather pants with a matching top. All of her rings and earrings are skulls. Her boots have about five inches of heels attached.

Rell steps a little closer. "Dee, is that you?" he asks.

She smiles and runs towards him with her arms wide apart. "Yes, it's me." She reaches him and hugs him tightly. "Yes, it's me...".

Chapter Twenty

The IAD had to halt the interrogation and read their informant his rights. They cannot take any chances. This case is too big to lose because of a few technicalities. They already know big lawyers will be swarming around this case like flies over a filthy trash can. They'll be plucking through everything until they find something that will get this entire case thrown out of court, before it even gets started.

Leaning forward, Detective Brown gets close to O'Miley's face. "Now that you know your rights, I need you to continue telling me about the Irish Blood!"

"Well," the informant clears his throat. "They're not exactly called the Irish Blood. I just call them that, because it is required that you be an Irish descendant to be trusted."

"Trusted?" Brown asks.

"Well, accepted into the circle," O'Miley clarifies.

Detective Riley cuts in. "All right, just tell us about the murders for now." Riley adjusts his seat. "Tell us about the rest of the killings that you're aware of."

The rookie sits back for a second, and then stares at the detective suspiciously. It takes only a few seconds for him to respond. "Okay, but the other murder was more gruesome." He takes another drink from his glass and clears his throat. "This time, Detective Ryan Brewkowski received a call from Terrell Jacobs' friend, Phillip Jenkins. Jenkins called my partner and everyone else in their little group and set up a plan to snatch him."

"Whoa!" Brown, the big detective, cuts in. "What type of call was it?" he asks.

"Mr. Jenkins was only trying to speak of his friend's innocence," O'Miley says.

Riley chimes in. "How did you know this?"

"Because they were all laughing about it when they tortured him." O'Miley drops his head.

He can't believe this is happening. It all seems like a dark, twisted dream from which he can't escape. "Because Phillip was screaming his friends' innocence while the Irish were killing him." He mumbles something, but no one understands what he says. "I'm sorry...". It's the only thing left he can manage to say.

"Okay, son, we really need you to keep yourself together so that we can help you." Big Joe pauses and gives the young cop time for the words to sink into his mind. After a minute or two passes, Brown pushes for more information. "All right, just tell us what happened when you guys met Mr. Jacobs, and how did he die?"

A flash of uncertainty appears across the wrinkles of O'Miley's face. He scrutinizes the two detectives before him. Then, he stares at the two-way mirror as if he could see straight through it. His throat is still dry. No matter how much water he drinks, he can't seem to rid that nasty, dry taste from his tongue.

He now wishes he had never come to speak to the detectives. He should've never said so much. However, he knows it's too late to undue everything that's been said. He's beyond knee deep. He's in way over his head, and now he feels like he's suffocating. It's too late. There's nowhere to go. It's too late. This is the closest he'll ever be to freedom again. Life is over for him. He knows that there are agents on the other side of that mirror who he'll be leaving with as soon as he finishes up his statement.

Taking a deep breath, he pleads with the detectives. "Listen, I can't go to prison." O'Miley looks around the small room. For what? He has no clue. "If I tell you everything, I need you guys to make sure I don't go to jail. If I go, they have friends in there who will kill me." His face tightens with anger and fear. "I can't help you people if you're going to leave me out to die," O'Miley says, matter-of-factly.

Tom cuts him off. "Hold up, guy. Don't forget, you're the one who came to us for help. With that being said though, we're not going to just forget that you stuck your neck out there to destroy this group of rogue cops." Riley relaxes his face to appear truly concerned. "We don't want you to spend a second in jail. It's not you we're after; we want them. So, please calm yourself down and tell us the rest of the story."

O'Miley's never been so afraid in his life. He's confused more than anything else. If he tells on his partners, he'll be forever branded an enemy of the force. Even worse, he'll be a disgrace to his family-especially his highly respected father. And... if he goes to prison, the prisoners will spend their whole time trying to kill him. He knows he's going to go to prison. However, the more information he gives on the other guys, the less time he'll have to do.

His bottom lip begins to quiver with fear. "I... we caught him at Liberty Park," he says.

The two detectives turn to one another. Joe asks, "Who asked to meet at Liberty Park?"

"He did. Phillip Jenkins." O'Miley waits to see if they respond, but they don't. They only take notes. The informant moves on with the story. "Since we caught him there, it was decided that was where we would dump his friend's wife's dead body."

Big Joe growls. His face starts to turn a bright crimson shade as he tries to keep himself from choking the little bastard. "But she didn't die! She lived! Guess that wasn't part of the plan, huh? So, whose idea was it to kill her and leave her out there?" Detective Brown is furious.

"She lived?" O'Miley whispers. His face is full of shock and disbelief. "How did she live through all of that?" His eyes were as big as saucers. He never imagined he would find out the woman was alive.

Giving Brown a second to cool down, Riley jumps back in the interrogation. "Son, we'll get back to that. Just tell us who decided to torture her like that. And then, you can get back to Jenkins' story."

"It was Detective Brewkowski. He planned it all." O'Miley keeps his head down, staring at the brown speckles in the linoleum floor.

"Hmm. . . you don't say." Big Joe glances to his partner.

O'Miley senses they don't believe him. He offers more information. "Once we grabbed Phillip Jenkins, we took him to an abandoned warehouse out by the docks." The kid quickly gives the location before the detectives even had time to ask for it. "When we caught him that morning, I knew that it would be a long day. I just wasn't expecting them to kill him, though." O'Miley looks up at the two detectives.

Brown and Riley only stare back at him with poker faces and wait for him to continue with his story.

"In our group, we have a few guys who are in the special forces- reserve, of course-but they know how to torture people without leaving any bruises or broken bones. They tied Jenkins down to an old hospital bed. I remember his feet were hanging over the edge. I didn't know what they were about to do, until..." O'Miley stops talking.

"Until what?" the Irish detective asks, starting to show some of his renowned fieriness.

"...until Detective Brewkowski walked in the building with that smirk on his face. He entered the room with this calmness that seemed so surreal. It was like he had no worry in the world. His demeanor gave me an uneasy feeling, but I was glad Brewkowski seemed to be in a normal frame of mind. I thought that he was only going to question him in order to bring Terrell Jacobs in. I couldn't have been more wrong." O'Miley drops his head again. He feels like it weighs a million pounds. He thought coming in to the station would lift some of the weight off of him, not add more to it.

Big Joe cuts back in. "Wait, I thought you said it was only Irish that could be in the group? Brewkowski's not Irish."

"You're right. That's the standard rule unless the group makes an exception. Brewkowski is German, but he wanted to be involved because O'Brien was his partner. Since he was such a loyal friend to O'Brien, and because he was always with O'Brien, we all agreed to let him join. It was easier that way, especially since O'Brien was in the group, and they were always together."

"Okay, back to Jenkins," Brown says, still writing things down on his pad.

"Brewkowski started by asking him where Terrell Jacobs was hiding out, but Phillip wouldn't tell him anything. After going back and forth for another five minutes, Brewkowski pulled out a thick broom handle that had been cut off from the bristlehead. He walked to the end of the hospital bed where Phillip's feet were hanging and asked him one more time for Terrell's location." Tilting his head, O'Miley takes a big breath before continuing the scene. "Phillip, again, pleaded for his friend's innocence, but it fell on deaf ears." Running his sweating hand through his clunky blond hair, O'Miley explains how Brewkowski reacted to Phillip's noncompliance. "Brewkowski stepped back, and just as if he were swinging a bat in a bat-cage, started beating the bottoms of Phillip's feet with that big broom stick."

The two detectives' eyes open wide with disbelief. They both know of this type of torture. It was used by the Chinese in the early ages. Even now, it's used in the Middle East to break down suspected terrorists so they'll give information. The only problem is that once someone hits a man with an object against the lower arc of the foot, the tortured individual is liable say absolutely anything to get the one beating them to stop. There have been reports of men begging to be shot, rather than go through such great pain.

Even the United States has been suspected of having secret prisons around the globe, utilizing these interrogation techniques., Because the pain is so great, it's virtually impossible to truly prove whether the accused individual or terrorist said certain things out of truth or just to try to prevent further torturing. On many accounts, the person being tortured has begged to be killed rather than continue.

The best thing about this type of torturing is that it leaves no wounds or any other visible sign of abuse. However, it does leave something far worse. It leaves the person who's been tortured on a lifelong carousel ride of horror. Many of the victims never fully recover. They report everything from sleepless nights to living in constant fear.

Brown snaps back to the matter at hand when he hears O'Miley talking again. "Suddenly, Jenkins started to speak. I guess he was in so much pain that he couldn't think right, because we barely could understand anything he said. Brewkowski walked around to the head of the bed and asked him to repeat what he had just said. . . ."

Detectives Riley and Brown remain stone faced as they wait for him to continue.

"Phillip Jenkins told us that Mr. Jacobs was hiding in Central Park," O'Miley says.

Glancing at the transparent mirror, O'Miley's voice gets quieter. "That's when Brewkowski went and got a couple of five-gallon buckets of water." Shaking his head, it's obvious O'Miley doesn't want to discuss the rest of what Brewkowski had done but proceeds nonetheless. "Brewkowski took his time, slowly pouring the water into Phillip's nostrils. Phillip Jenkins twisted his neck back and forth as much as he could, but his head and body were tightly secured to. Brewkowski drowned him right there on that hospital bed. It was a nightmare. It's still a nightmare. I can't get it out of my mind. I never seen a man drown before, especially on land." O'Miley looks completely drained as he finishes retelling the events of Phillip Jenkins' death.

After he tells the detectives about how they got rid of the body, Big Joe goes back over the facts of the case. Most importantly, Joe tries to think of how they can verify that this guy is telling the truth. He wants to make certain this case does not get messed up.

Regarding the two men in the car accident- Reyquan Lewis and Carlos Martinez- in order to confirm their deaths were indeed due to strangulation, their bodies can be reexamined to look for glove or hand print marks or indentions around their necks. If the killer didn't use gloves, then they might even find some viable fingerprint indentions, too. For Phillip Jenkins, they'll need to check his legs and arms for restraints marks. If he was in fact, drowned on land that can be proven by an autopsy. It's referred to as "dry drowning" and it can be determined by the amount of fluid within the lungs. But what if all of this was already taken care of? I mean, Brewkowski is a cop. What if he covered all of his tracks to where nothing points back to him? What if the two in the car were choked with their seat belt? What if Phillip Jenkins was tied down by an entire blanket being strapped down over his entire body? Big Joe is a little worried because these guys know how to evade the police...because they work for the law themselves.

Chapter Twenty-One

Supreme just stands there and stares as Rell and the woman hug each other tightly. He's wondering how and where this odd pair had even met each other. A banker and a rock band groupie. To him, it doesn't make any since. He knows his friend was having major marriage problems, but a hard-core rocker... Preme shakes his head.

Suddenly, the two begin passionately kissing each other. Supreme rolls his eyes and heads for the door. He's so confused by what's happening at the moment. Better yet, he's confused by everything that's happened recently. "I'm out y'all!" he says as he crosses the threshold.

The door sounds off as it hits its frame. The two glance back to make sure that he left.

Rell gazes down at her glowing face. "I can't believe you're here. I thought that I'd never see you again." He smiles from ear to ear.

Dee reaches up his tall frame, interlocks her fingers behind his head, and pulls him to her until his lips touch hers. "I miss you so much," she says, kissing him again.

Pulling away, Rell catches his breath. "Hold up, Dee. We really need to talk, first," he says.

She kisses him again before stepping back just a hair. "I don't want to talk right now," she says. She reaches for his belt buckle. "I need you." Pulling the belt from his pants, she makes sure he understands her intentions. "I need you badly," she whispers.

He stops her. He's a tad bit irritated by how flippant she is being about his current situation. "Do you realize how serious this it?" he asks her.

"Yes, I do, and I have some information that can save you." Dee waits for a reaction but gets none.

"You're not going to jail," she says.

His eyes open wide. "You're serious?" he asks. Okay, now she has his attention, but avoids any more chatter on the topic.

She ignores his question and begins unbuttoning his shirt while rubbing his rock hard chest. "Huh?" she says, playing stupid.

Rell repeats himself. "I said, 'Are you serious?'"

Groping his muscular pecs as she kisses and licks them, she finally answers him. "Yes, I'm very serious. I wouldn't lie to you. I know some police who will testify in court on your behalf." She licks his lower stomach as she pulls his penis out. She gazes up at him and tries to convince him of other things on her mind. "Now, let's not talk. Let's just show each other how much we've missed each other." Sucking the head of his limp manhood for a couple seconds, she tries another tactic to get him in the mood. "Don't be so stressed. Give me what I want and then I'll give you everything you need." Dee knows she's breaking his defenses, because he's literally growing in her hands. "Ooh, I love you so much," she says as his dick gets harder and harder.

She begins to suck his cock while simultaneously pulling her pants down. Rell, has given in. He grabs the back of her head and begins to ram himself deeper and deeper into her throat.

Dee's really aroused by this change of event- even though she had known he would eventually cave in to her- and begins to suck him even harder. "Wait," she says. She stands to her feet and quickly steps out of her pants. Before Rell can even take a breath, there's not a stitch of clothing left on her curvy, svelte frame.

Her petite body is so sexy, even though she's slightly bow-legged. Her breasts are more than a handful, and her pussy is shaved completely smooth.

Rell squeezes her ass he sits back on the couch. He knows what she wants, and he knows how to give it to her. Reaching out for her waist, he turns her body around to face away from him and opens his legs wide.

Dee smiles while looking over her shoulder. She knows what her lover is about to give her, and it's well worth the wait.

Pulling her back, he gently guides her body until she is sitting on his erect member. It slides into her with such ease, like it was meant to be there. She feels so warm and incredibly tight on the inside; he wants to cum now, but he refuses to. He wants to give her everything she needs and could ever ask for.

Leaning forward, Dee folds her arms on top of the coffee table and rests her face on the folded makeshift pillow. She raises her back to form an arch and begins to slowly thrust back to her man.

She does it slowly so that his penis rubs against her g-spot. He only had to show her once what she had been missing out on. Now, she wants it like this just about all of the time.

He reaches around her waist, gently feeling his way toward the warmth only inches away from his hand. He begins to stroke her clitoris with his index finger as she continues to arch her back. As they like to say, he's giving her his "double dose". The faster she thrusts back, the faster he strokes her throbbing clit.

He opens his legs even wider to allow her maximum access to the extent of his large penis.

"Tell me baby: You love this dick don't you?" Rell asks her.

Her breath is fast, and her speech is raspy. "Oh, yes, Rell! Oh yes! I love that big dick, baby."

Rubbing her clitoris faster, Rell is on cloud nine. "Fuck me baby. Fuck the shit out of this dick. Show me how much you missed me." Humping back to meet her soaking wet pussy, Rell begs for an orgasm. "C'mon baby, fuck me... Fuck me. Make me cum..."

She's in such a world of bliss, her tongue seems to be in a choke hold. "Oooo, Reeeeellll, baaaaay – beeee. . . oooooh, yes. Fuuuuuck meeeeee," she says. It's music to Rell's ears.

She must have really missed him, because she's already about to have another orgasm. She slows just a bit, but she refuses to stop. A thick, white fluid is dripping from her juicy insides. Yes, she came and will again.

Rell only slows to match her pace, but he can't stop. He still wants her as bad as she wants him. He's holding his muscles tightly, because he doesn't want to cum... not yet. It feels too good to him. Her insides are so warm and wet.

Only a minute later, and she's speeding up again. She's pushing her body back against his shaft as hard as possible. She wants all of him inside her.

Rell grips her butt cheeks tighter as he spreads them apart so that he can give her all of his big dick that she wants.

Dee pushes herself up from the table as she continues to ride him. She stops for a second to turn around and face her love.

Rell doesn't stop. He fucks her even harder now that he's staring her in her eyes.

The two begin to passionately kiss as they make love and fuck at the same time.

She's cumming all over the couch. It's all thick and creamy. She knows she hasn't cummed like this in a very long time...possibly since the last time she was with Rell.

She leans in closer. "Cum inside of me, Rell," she whispers in his ear. Tightening her vagina's inner muscles, she rides him even harder. "Cum inside, baby."

Rell stops trying to hold back. It feels too good to block it off any longer. He begins to pump even harder. She feels so good to him when she tightens her insides.

He grunts, "Uh –I'm about to cum!"

Pulling his head in, she locks her tongue around his as she thrusts her waist harder and harder against his cumming cock.

Chapter Twenty-Two

The rookie finishes his glass of water. "Excuse me. I need to use the bathroom."

Both detectives take sips from their cups of fresh, hot coffee at the same time as if they were synchronized divers or something. Neither of the two respond to his request.

"Excuse me... I need to use the bathroom!" O'Miley says, louder this time.

Big Joe sits his cup down. "Listen, son, we'll take you to the restroom once we hear Sheila Jacobs' story."

Shaking his head, O'Miley knows arguing is a lost cause. "You guys, I can see that this is going to be a wonderful friendship," he sarcastically says. Frustration flashes across O'Miley's face as he leans back in his chair. "We followed her to Phillip

Jenkin's place.   We searched his place and didn't find anything..." O'Miley quickly stands up, shoving the table at them in the process. His face is blazing red. "Look, I have to use the fucking bathroom!" He's not saying anything else until they let him take a piss.

Someone knocks on the window.   Big Joe sighs and then waves his hand to the person straddling the threshold. "All right.   Take him to the rest room." The detectives know they won't get anywhere by letting O'Miley piss on himself.

O'Miley is taken to the restroom and returns in less than ten minutes.   The two detectives are already becoming frustrated by his bathroom outburst, but time is against them and they still don't want to mess this up.

Coming back, the rookie sits with a smirk of arrogance on his face and jumps right back into his story. "We took Terrell Jacobs' wife with us. Once we got her to our safe area-"

Detective Riley cuts him off. "Explain, safe area," he says.

O'Miley obliges. "It's a location that's been cleared of all patrol cars. We have a few friends' up at dispatch and they clear the area whenever needed."

"Okay. Continue." Riley rolls his eyes like a teenage girl.

"We made her talk," O'Miley says.

Big Joe cuts in. "Yeah, you made her talk. Who decided to abuse her and rape her?" he asks.

Suddenly, O'Miley is tripping over his words, talking a mile a minute. "It was Brewkowski. First, he raped her and then he beat her badly with sticks, and later he smashed in her skull at the park."

The detectives can't hide their feelings. Their faces are in tight knots. Each is looking like they want to kill him.

"You see...Brewkowski has this thing for black women, but he says he hates them," O'Miley tells them.

"What thing?" Riley asks.

"Well, he's turned on by them, but he doesn't want anyone to know – but it's clearly obvious that he's into those spooks." The words slip out before he's able to control his thoughts. His eyes open wide as he covers his mouth with his hand. "Oops, excuse me. I didn't mean to say that."

Big Joe gives a fake grin. "Yeah, we understand son."

"Brewkowski injected her with a strong dose of heroin. After it took its affect, he forced his way inside of her. She begged and fought as much as possible, but between the powerful drugs and him, it was useless. He did as he pleased with her and then after, he beat her like a man who killed his mother." O'Miley glances across the table, finally looking up from the speck of dirt he had been talking to. "That's Brekowski's problem. He hates himself for craving black women, and he doesn't want anyone to know. We all have known for some time now, though. He's been raping black women for years."

Tom fires off. "For years?" he asks.

O'Miley replies. "Yes, for many years. Before I even joined the force."

Big Joe's face is painted with anger and sorrow. "Son, just tell us how this all happened and how you can prove. Terrell Jacobs' innocence."

"Well, it all started when O'Brien hired a private detective to see if his wife was having an affair. It only took a few weeks for the P.I. to come back with an answer. She was having an affair." Running his fingers threw his hair for the thousandth time, O'Miley kept talking. "He couldn't accept the fact that his young beautiful wife was having an affair with that spook. . . Terrell Jacobs."

Chapter Twenty-Three

She comes from the bathroom with a towel wrapped around her body and another one wrapped around her head. Debbie O'Brien's face is glowing with satisfaction. She goes over to the couch and picks up her jacket. She retrieves an envelope from a secret pocket that she had cut inside the lining of the back of the jacket.

She walks over to Rell. "Here you go dear," she says, handing him the envelope.

"What's this?" Rell asks.

"Just open it and read it," she says.

Rell takes the envelope. He stares at her as he slowly opens it. After pulling the tape off of the seal, he tilts his chin down and continues to open the envelope.

Debbie speaks softly. "When I was at his funeral, a private detective brought that to me. He told me that Marten had had someone watching us since the very beginning of our affair. But, when the PI turned the evidence over to my husband Marten, he could tell that Marten wasn't concerned with a divorce; he knew that Marten only wanted to kill the black man who his wife was in love with." Debbie stops long enough to let everything sink in. She knows it won't take Rell long now to put the pieces together.

Rell slowly glances up to her and then looks back down to the contents inside of the envelope. He feels the room closing in on him; the room is getting hot again, but in no way like it had been an hour ago. There's photos taken at his bank from the first month when they decided to see each other. Then, there's what seems like a million pictures of them sneaking into various hotel rooms. So many nights they spent together, at least partially. He pauses as he holds one picture closer to his face. He remembers this one. It all makes sense now. "This was the night that someone kept knocking on the door to our room and then running off. Damn, I was set up. The PI took pictures whenever I opened the door."

Next, Rell pulls out a few pictures from the night of the murder. He immediately recognizes himself and Marten O'Brien; the picture shows them fighting in the rain.

Holding the picture up, Rell's face appears confused again. He looks to Dee. "How did he get these?" he asks.

Debbie's face looks reassuring. She knows he's probably experiencing some type of shock. "That's what I was telling you a few minutes ago. The PI told me that he didn't trust Marten, so he had continued to follow him around after he had given him the evidence against us." Debbie walks over and wraps her arms around her love. She doesn't know if he's ready to hear what she's about to tell him next. "So because the PI was following Marten that night, the PI really has all of the proof to save you. He followed Marten and the rest of them to that bar you and your friends were at. The PI watched them the whole time. He even saw them kill Reyquan and Carlos."

"They killed them? Rell asks. The police?" Rell's eyes seem so distant as he talks.

"Yes, and the PI has all of the proof. This is why he's been in hiding, too." Debbie is trying to be as positive and sensitive as she can. She knows she's unloading so much information on him right now. She lets him take his time.

"They killed Reyquan and Carlos." A painful tear leaks from his eye and slowly rolls down his check. "I can't believe all of this is because of me," he says. Pushing her away, a stern and serious look suddenly appears on his face. "You must leave...right now. I want you to go to the police. No, this is their fault to begin with. I mean, you gotta go to the FBI or something." Shit, he's so overwhelmed.

Debbie knows she can't keep the panic out of her voice much longer. "Wait Rell. Are you listening? They're looking for me, too. They want to kill me, too. Why do you think I dyed my hair black and purple and was dressed like a punk rocker when I got here tonight? I'm scared for my life, too." Debbie begins to weep. "I don't want to die, either."

He realizes what she's saying is so true and tries to calm her down. "Wait, I didn't mean it that way. I'm just as worried for your life as I am my own. Right now, I'm not sure what these people might do."

Rell takes a moment to run through everything in his head.. "Now, I have to deal with the Italian mob and the Jersey City police department...wait until Supreme hears this. He's going to go crazy, but then again, I'm the cause of most of this and I can't drag him into anymore of my mess." Rell decides his pep talk didn't do his mind much pepping', so to speak.

Pulling herself back to her love, Debbie sees the hurt and fear in his eyes. She wants to take all the bad away. "Rell, don't push me away right now.

Not when we need each other the most." She kisses him. "Rell, I need you too badly. I need you," she whispers.

This time, Rell kisses back and rips the towel from her body. He grabs her right thigh and raises it just enough to open the smooth, pink slits between her legs. It seems like his throbbing, hard dick has a mind of its own, because it finds its way inside of her without the guidance from his hands.

Within seconds, she hops off of the floor with her other leg and wraps both of them around his waist.

He grabs her ass cheeks as he lifts and drops her on his stiff rod. Oh, there's no doubt- his mission is to fuck the shit out of her.

Debbie clutches her arms around the back of his neck, using it like a handle so that she can ride the hell out of him. She uses her legs as support around his waist to hop higher and higher. Her pussy is so fucking wet. She's dripping all over him. Her thick cum is running down his thighs and dripping from his testicles.

He kisses her as he moves his hand to her breast. He gropes her like never before. Moving from her lips, his tongue slowly travels down the tip of her chin and leaves a trail of goosebumps as it travels down her neck before reaching her erect nipples. He sucks them, gently licks them, and then moves back up to her neck where he begins to lick and suck that secret tender spot that drives her wild. Wait, he goes back to her nipples. Her stiff, erect nipples drive him absolutely insane.

He's licking in a circular motion while groping them ever so softly, listening to the soft moans escaping her lips.

With his other hand, he rubs the inside ridges of her juicy pussy. His hand quickly fills with her cum.

Debbie clenches his hard, muscle-bound back firmly. She wants to dig into his flesh with her nails so badly, but she knows he doesn't like that. Hold up, her face suddenly drops deep into his neck.

She moans and groans with pleasure. "Ooh, stop... Wait..." she says.

Rell knows what it means, and he follows her wish.

The two are locked in their position. He's standing, holding her in mid-air.

She's trembling with ecstasy. A thick, white foam is seeping from her satisfied, sweet, hot, passionate body.

After a few moments, she lifts her head and unwraps herself from his waist. "Now, let me please you," she says, starry-eyed and eager. Getting down on her knees, she grabs his shaft before looking back up to his face. "Cum in my mouth," she tells him.

Without hesitation, she places his penis between her perky breasts as he begins to pump. She licks and sucks the head of his manhood with his every stroke.

Rell grabs the back of her head and does his best to put everything he has down her throat. He knows that she loves this, because she knows how to deep throat all nine inches of him. Thank Goodness, she doesn't have a gag reflex. He grins to himself as he watches her do her magic.

Debbie releases her breasts and begins to take more and more down her throat. The head of his penis is rubbing against her tonsils. She knows this is his weakness.

Her ability to deep throat has him going crazy inside of his mind.

He mutters, "Ugh, Imma 'bout to cum."

She squeezes her own breasts to further arouse herself for his thick cum. His knees buckle before he goes. She grabs his dick with her other hand and strokes it to ensure that everything spurts out directly into her hungry throat. Her eyes glow with joy.

Chapter Twenty-Four

"*Wow!*" Tom exclaims. Rubbing his chin, he repeats, "Wow!" They're having an affair!"

He looks to his partner with disbelief, because all along he and Big Joe had thought that it was Detective Brewkowski who was having the affair.

Still rubbing his chin, Tom pops the big question. "Who's the P.I.?"

"I don't know, but I do know that they're still looking for him because they don't want him to talk," O'Miley says.

Tom glances to his partner, trying to gauge if Big Joe also thinks O'Miley is lying. "Hmm, is that so?" Tom asks, again.

O'Miley knows the detectives don't believe him, yet. "Yes, they're also following Debbie O'Brien to find Mr. Jacobs. They placed a triangulation on her phone to maintain her whereabouts." Neither detective says a word. "And that is why I'm here, because if you guys don't intervene, they will kill Terrell and Debbie both."

"Kill them both?" Big Joe questions.

"Yes, Mr. Jacobs called her last night, and they set up a rendezvous for this morning. When they meet, they will be snatched and murdered."

The detectives stand to their feet, simultaneously asking the pertinent question. "Where are the two of them located?" they ask.

Suddenly, the door bursts open. It's the rookie's father, followed by one of those fancy attorneys. The detectives already know the game's about to change completely.

The rookie's father places his hand on his son's shoulder. "Son, don't say anything else. We need to have you see a psychologist before you talk with these wonderful people," he says.

The lawyer steps around to the other side of O'Miley. He sets his briefcase down and hands each of the detectives his business card. "My client has nothing else to say, and whatever was said isn't valid, because he has a diminished capacity.

"Crazy!" Tom yells as he stands up.

Big Joe glances to his partner first before looking the attorney dead in his eyes. "He may be a lot of things, but crazy is not one of them," he says.

Tom cuts back in before the attorney gets a chance to respond.. "Do you realize that there are people who may die if he doesn't tell us where they're located?"

The father becomes belligerent. "I don't give a damn about what you say! My son is going with me!" he shouts.

Several other agents run from the observation room to aid the two IAD detectives, who are about to be attacked by O'Miley's unruly father.

The room is immediately crowded as they all surrounded the attorney and the over excited father. The father raises his arms like he's about to attack. Before they're halfway up, he's tackled.

Amongst all the confusion, someone enters the tiny room filled with people and taps Big Joe. Big Joe steps out to the hallway for a brief second. Whoever it was gave him a piece of paper with a number on it. Glancing back to the confusion in the interrogation room, he decides that everything is okay and goes to the nearest land line to call the number.

Inside the room, the father and son are both in handcuffs. The attorney has been shoved back into a corner. Three IAD agents, along with two FBI agents, are now in the room with Detective Tom Riley.

Staring the father dead in his eyes, Tom tries to convey the urgency of the situation. "Do you not understand how serious this is? I can't believe that you were a decorated law officer – and now, you'd allow something like this to go so far?" Leaning closer to his huffing and puffing opponent, he keeps on talking. "Either you can stand in the way and go to jail with your son, or you can get him to talk and, possibly, we can at least get the both of you some help." Tom glares at him, waiting for a response.

The highly decorated retired lieutenant says nothing. He only stares Tom back down.

"Oh, I see you have nothing to say. Hmm, well, your fancy attorney needs to remind you that under the Patriot Act, you and the rest of the Irish in your group can be classified as a terrorist group. With that being said, we don't have to give you nor your son the right to speak with an attorney just yet." Looking over the father's shoulder, Tom has asked a sidebar question to an FBI agent. "What? We can hold him for several years until we get to the bottom of this, huh?" Detective Tom Riley is pretty sure he's got his point across to the father.

Pink blots of fear spot up the father's cheeks. He looks over his shoulder to his attorney.

The attorney and one of the FBI agents both nod their heads.

Tom continues, "And if you think you can still afford this expensive lawyer – don't worry, because we'll definitely freeze all of your accounts and assets until this case is over."

The father only stares blankly.

Big Joe walks back into the room. His face is different. It's blank with shock and grief. He closes the door behind himself and steps away from it. If the kid and his father thought the detectives were serious earlier, they have no idea what's around the corner. Big Joe will get answers...and soon.

He leans on the small table. The legs tremble under his massive frame. He ignores everyone in the room except the rookie. "You know your time is about to run out. Sheila Jacobs just died at the hospital." Leaning even closer, Brown's eyes shoot daggers at O'Miley. "Only you described how she was killed. Only you described every homicide that has been committed during this entire investigation. So, that only leaves you to convict," Detective Brown says, turning to the young cop's father. "So, no matter what attorney you bring in this room or building, he'll be doing a lot of time-unless he gives us the information we need to save some lives." Big Joe's shaking because he's so angry.

Suddenly, Big Joe's cell phone begins to vibrate.

The rookie begins to speak.

The big guy only holds up his pointer finger, indicating for him to wait a second.

Joe answers his phone. "Yes," he says flatly into the receiver. He's quiet as he listens to the person on the other end. "Thanks!" he says. He glances at the rookie, while still on the phone. "Please, call me back if anything changes." Ending his call, Big Joe turns to his partner. "Put your coat and vest on," he says.

Tom Riley jumps to his feet and runs out the door. "I'll meet you at the car, Joe."

The rookie begins to speak, but Joseph Brown cuts him off. "It's too late, son," he says. Heading out the door, Detective Joe Brown glances to the agents standing around. "You guys can book them both. We're done here. They had their chance," he says.

First, he runs to his cubicle to grab his coat and vest. Big Joe yells up the hall to his partner and asks him to hold the elevator door. After grabbing his badge from his desk, he races for the elevator.

The two wait for the elevator door to close before they talk. Tom presses the button for the first floor. He steps back, leans against the wall, and stares at Big Joe.

Big Joe waves him off. "C'mon man. You know it was easy to get her location since her phone is already being triangulated. She's in Harlem. I just want us to get a head start. I asked to be the first to know."

Chapter Twenty-Five

After their third sexual escapade in the shower, Rell and Debbie have a seat on the couch and review all of the evidence that the private investigator had given her at the funeral.

It turns out that the PI had far more than what Rell and Debbie had expected. He even had photos of the rogue cops when they snatched Sheila from Phillip's building.

All of this is too much for Rell. Even though he had seen them throw her into that car, he wasn't able to see the up-close details of his wife's face. She was terrified for her life, but she still never told her kidnappers that Rell was so close.

Rell can feel his eyes start to tear up. He quickly drops the picture to the table and falls back to the couch. He covers his eyes to block the tears from falling down his cheeks. His head is throbbing with an indescribable aching pain. It's like a heartache traveling from his chest to his head. It's just too much.

Debbie wraps her arms around his neck and rests her head on his shoulder. She speaks so softly. "Don't worry. We're going to get all of them for what they did," she says.

Shaking his head, Rell knows she has no clue what he's feeling. "No, you don't understand. I caused all of this. I placed my family in harm's way. I placed you in harm's way, too." Rell feels so much pain but feels so empty at the same time.

She leans away and frowns. "One moment, what? You didn't do anything to me that I didn't do to myself. I wanted you just as bad as you wanted me," she says.

The phone rings.

They both freeze momentarily until they realize it's the apartment phone.

After recognizing the number on the caller ID, Rell reaches for the phone. "It's okay, Debbie. It's Supreme." He places the ear piece against his head. "Hello," Rell says. He listens contently. "Ah man, not him again, Preme. I'm not really in the mood for that crazy old man. I still want to get him back for hitting me," he replies.

Rell doesn't say much more before reluctantly hanging up the phone.

Debbie's face is worried. "What's wrong? What was all that about?" she asks.

Rell brings her up to speed. "That's about this old bastard, goes by the name Ole Man, who punched me in my mouth last night. Supreme is sending him down to give us something to eat. He said that it's some curry chicken."

She lightly frowns with perplexity. "Okay, what's so wrong with that?" she asks. Her face wrinkles a bit more. "And, he punched you in the face?"

"You don't understand. That ole geezer is crazy." Rell pauses. "Wait – you should hurry and put your clothes back on. He's also an old pervert. He won't even leave if he sees you like this."

She smiles. "Are you worried that he may take me from you?" she says, teasing him.

He smiles and then the thoughts of his wife and children flash through his head. The sadness has returned. "I don't think he can afford your full package."

She hurts for him. "Rell, I'm so sorry, too. I am as guilty as you, maybe even more than you. I saw you and wanted you far before you even recognized me. I knew you were having marriage problems because Sue, who works for you at the bank, told me about your problems- and I didn't even care. I just wanted you in my arms from the moment that I first saw you." Holding her head down, Debbie continues her confession. "I knew my marriage was over years ago. I just wanted you."

Rell gives a faint smile. "It's all okay, Debbie," he says. Don't worry about any of that now, just get dressed before that old man gets down here."

She wants to continue on the subject, but she knows it's not the right time.

She bows her head lightly. "Okay Rell."

He watches her walk away as he moves for the front door. He wants to keep an eye on the peep hole, just to make sure that he catches Ole Man at the door. He only wants to open it long enough to grab the food, and that's it.

Staring through the peep hole, he realizes why Supreme chose this apartment. It's at the end of the hallway and everything in the hall can be clearly seen through the peephole. Rell can see that there's a guy from the power company talking to a man at an apartment door. There's a couple with an infant opening their door to get in their apartment.

Debbie calls his name.

"Hmm!" is all he says. He doesn't want to yell while at the door.

She comes out, and tries again. "I said, what are you doing?"

Rell whispers, "Nothing. I'm just watching the hall."

"Why are you watching the hall and whispering like that?" she asks.

"Shh!" he says, waving her off.

He sees Ole Man coming off of the elevator with the food in his hands.

The power company guy passes over the clip board as Ole Man passes by them.

Rell cracks the door open as soon as Ole Man steps within three feet of it.

Rell reaches out for the food, but Ole Man steps away from Rell's outstretched hand.

"Uh-uh, I want to see the snow bunny you got in there," Ole Man says.

Rell whispers, "C'mon Ole Man, we don't have any time for this. Stop playing."

Ole Man tightens his grip on the bags. "Let me see her, or I'll take the food with me. I ain't playing, Rell." The old bastard looks as serious as a heart attack.

Rell squeezes the opening of the door to the point to where only Rells' eyes can be seen. "Well, fuck you then. You old bastard," he says through clenched teeth.

He tries to close the door, but Ole Man stops it with his foot. "Now you're learning, son." The mean old man pushes the door a bit. "Here's your food," he says.

Rell takes the food and closes the door.

Debbie quickly comes over to grab the food, and then heads toward the kitchen with the two bags.

She calls out to Rell while preparing the food for the microwave. "I'll have everything ready in a few minutes," she says.

Rell doesn't say anything. He has his eyeball glued to the peep hole. He's watching Ole Man haphazardly make his way down the hall, singing an old slow song from his youth. He can't decipher the exact song, but it sounds like it's one of those Temptation's songs.

Rell really wants to run out there and punch his old ass in the back of the head, but Rell knows he'll only feel guilty afterwards.

As Ole Man passes the guy from the power company and the man at the door, they both stare at him.

Wait. Shit, shit, shit. Rell runs to the table and searches through the photos.

He quickly sees the one that he's looking for. It's the photo with 'Brewkowski' written on the back of it. He runs back over to the door and presses his eye against the peep hole again.

Yep, just like he thought; it's him. . . Brewkowski. Fear smacks Rell right in his chest, but he keeps himself under full control. The confusion pops up out of nowhere and leaves him standing in a world of perplexity.

Suddenly, he finds his voice. He whispers, "Dee, get out here, now."

She's in the kitchen, but still manages to hear him. "Hmm?" she asks.

Again, he whispers, "Get out here now." His voice is stern. He refuses to remove his eye from peep hole. "Dee, we have to get out of here, now," he says.

Debbie comes from around the corner, huffing and puffing in a state of fear.

"What's wrong?" she asks.

"Those cops are outside," he says.

The panic creeps into Debbie's voice. "What are we going to do?"

Quickly glancing back, Rell responds. "We're getting out of here." Turning back to the peephole, he realizes something else. "They're starting to group up," he says.

More of the crooked cops begin to come out of the apartment door where Brewkowski had been standing. They must have tied up the family that lives there... or either they killed them.

Without turning his head, Rell points to the window with the fire escape attached to it. "Open it," he says. His hands are shaking. "Wait! Debbie, make sure that no one is out there, first." Even though he is trying to appear calm, Rell feels like he's losing control on the inside.

Debbie looks out the window. "I don't see anyone," she says. She opens the window and sticks her head out. "Rell, there's no one out here."

Holding his position against the peephole, Rell plans their next move. "Okay, bring me the phone really quick," he says.

She does just that..

Without his eye still pressing against the peephole, Rell calls Supremes' phone. It rings twice before Supreme answers.

Rell doesn't give him the chance to say much. He cuts Preme off as he whispers. "Preme, they're here."

Supreme pulls out his other phone. "Those Italians?" he asks.

Rell tries to say as much as he can with as few words as possible. "No. It's the dirty cops. They're the ones who killed everyone."

Rell can vaguely hear Supreme telling someone on his other phone to go tell everyone to get their weapons ready.

Rell's voice is super low. "Preme, do you hear me?" he asks.

Supreme tries to reassure his friend. "Yes, I hear you and get down on the floor, because we're coming ...we're coming down now."

"Oh shit, Preme, they're coming toward the door." Rell's breathing accelerates to the point he's almost panting "Oh shit! Man, I'm climbing out to the fire escape." That's the last thing Supreme hears from Rell.

Rell drops the phone and runs to the window. Debbie is already climbing to the floor below. She started moving as soon as he said, "oh shit".

As soon as he gets one leg out of the window, the door is kicked down. Rell looks Brewkowski straight in the eyes. The staring contest lasts less than a split second, but it seems like an eternity. Brewkowski takes aim for Rell's head, but Rell drops out of the window sill like a wet sack of rocks.

He lands on the metal floor of the fire escape. Quickly, he rolls over and jumps down the flight of stairs. Rell glides his hands down over the railing to keep from falling over as he hits the floor below.

Landing on his feet, he looks Debbie in her eyes. Without looking back, he knows Brewkowski is overhead. He knows it by the pure fear exuding from Debbie's eyes.

Suddenly, sounds of fire balls are shooting from the floor above. Brrrrrrr – brrrrrr – brrrrrr! They came with fully automatic assault rifles.

Rell has been away from the grimy streets for many years now, but he could never forget the sound of a fully automatic AR -15. He grabs Debbie and pulls her close. He makes sure to shield her body as he jumps through a nearby apartment window. They land in a bed of shredded glass on the floor.

While on the kitchen floor of the apartment, he hears the footsteps of Brewkowski racing down the stairs of the fire escape.

Jumping to his feet, Rell goes to lift Debbie by grabbing her arm. It's too late. In the corner of his eye, he sees Brewkowski taking aim from outside the window. Rell tenses his body in preparation for the impact of bullets that are inevitably coming his way.

Chapter Twenty-Six

Ryan Brewkowski leans into the window frame as he stares down the barrel of his gun to his target, Terrell Jacobs. Ryan Brewkowski smiles deep within his soul, because he's about to end this wild game of cat and mouse. He thinks back to his partner O'Brien, and how O'Brien would basically have a royal flush in his hand, and accidentally fold instead of bid. Even when things were right where they should be, O'Brien still got it all wrong.

His partner could have easily killed Rell that night, but he was drunk. O'Brien started drinking pretty heavily every since he and Debbie began having marriage problems. O'Brien had everything in the right place, but he was too drunk. He couldn't even stand up straight; however, Brewkowski didn't realize this until it was too late. By the time Brewkowski had realized how far gone his partner was, O'Brien was in the middle of the ally, struggling to draw his pistol.

In only milliseconds, Brewkowski's mind flashes back to another guy who he had killed just last year. He and Rell look just alike. The only difference is that the other guy was a filthy drug dealing snitch who was about to testify on Brewkowski and his partner for taking bribes to drop some burglary cases.

Brewkowski reveals a smirk as he clutches the trigger. His target? Terrell Jacobs' head.

Rell flinches at the sight of the gun. He waits, knowing what's coming.

A scream is heard in the back ground. It's Debbie.

Wait – there's another voice, too. One of the dirty cops has been hit. He's yelling for help. He's about to where Brewkowski is standing. The cop is going to fall over the fire escape railing. He tripped when the bullet hit him in his side.

Brewkowski drops everything and runs up to his friend. But, before he gets to him, the gun fire erupts... Boom! Boom! A shotgun blows the cop over the railing. Brewkowski hears his friend's screams for help as his friend drops ten stories down.

Brewkowski retrieves his weapon. Rell and Debbie are gone. He glances back to his crew, and then he climbs into the window. He moves swiftly, but with caution at the same time. Another guy jumps in behind him.

A total of five of the dirty cops make it out from the apartment above. Two are wounded. One was hit in his leg and the other was grazed on the chin. They're both bleeding badly. There were eight of them.

One cop yells, "They're coming down the fire escape!"

Brewkowski and his team run out of the kitchen and post up in the next room. They wait for some of the guys to climb into the kitchen window before they start to shower the kitchen with melting hot lead.

Brewkowski pats one of his men on the shoulder, signaling for him to go with him. He and his cohort run out of the apartment's front door. As soon as they step into the hall, the officer with Brewkowski spots Debbie following Rell down the staircase. They give chase.

The dirty cops weren't able to bring their usual gadgets and toys to the "raid", because they're not supposed to be here. They can't allow this to look like a typical police raid; that type of raid would have to be backed up by tons of paperwork. They want it to look like a drug deal gone bad or a violent neighborhood robbery.

Brewkowski sees him. He takes aim at Rell. It's a difficult shot, but there's no time to doubt his skills. He shoots sporadically. Rell's body falls over.

Chapter Twenty-Seven

The IAD detectives, Joseph Brown and Tom Riley, are only a few blocks away from the location. Big Joe's phone rings.

He answers, "Yeah." Glancing to Tom, he acknowledges what the caller is telling him. "Mmm-hmm, alright," Big Joe says. He ends the call and lets out a heavy sigh. "Well, ole-buddy-ole-pal," he says to Tom, "things just got that much worse."

"What's wrong now?" Tom asks.

Placing his phone back in his pocket, Detective Brown fills Tom in. "Earlier, before we left, remember when I was checking on the location on Debbie O'Brien's phone? Well, I also placed a triangulation signal on Brewkowski's phone." His face wrinkles. "And guess what?" he asks.

As soon as they hit the corner of the location, Brown and Riley notice that the street is a bit empty for a regular New York day. The only people outside are all standing around a vehicle.

They pull their car next to the crowd who is gathered around the silver Infinity truck. Once they slow their car, the crowd recognizes they're law enforcement and disperses.

Tom sees the dead body that the crowd had been looking at. "OH, don't tell me – Brewkowski is here, too, huh?" he asks his partner.

Big Joe frowns. "Yep."

The IAD detectives park their car and jump out.

Walking across the street, Tom calls out to an old lady. She walks away for a few more feet before she turns around and begins to walk toward the officers. Another lady calls out to her and she then begins to walk away from the IAD.

Tom calls out to her, again. "Ma'am, could you please tell me what happened out here?" he asks.

She points up to the sky. "He just fell. What the fuck else you need to know?" she says, obviously in no mood to have a discussion with him.

Shaking his head, Tom backs off. "Ma'am, thank you for your time anyway."

From above, the shooting starts up again. The two detectives duck behind the Infinity truck.

Big Joe quickly reaches up to the dead guy laying on the truck and searches him. He grabs something and squats back down again. "Just like I thought," he says. Big Joe holds the badge up for Tom to see. "I thought he looked familiar," Joe says.

Tom grins. He says, "I wonder how Brewkowski and his crew expect to clean all of this up. If they can do that, they're better than Harry Houdini the magician."

The IAD duo radio back to their boss and request for back up. Their captain informs them to stay put and wait for the FBI and local authorities to arrive at the scene.

The two check each other for a certain facial expression. They want to make sure that they both agree that there is no time to waste. If they're going to be in the doghouse, the decision to disobey a direct command has to be mutual. They know that Brewkowski is trying to make sure that Terrell Jacobs never gets the word out that Jacob's has been nothing but a pawn in this fucked up world of confusion. Plus, if Jacob's ever makes it to court, Brewkowski knows Terrell Jacob's would be the prosecutor's king on the stand.

Suddenly, they charge toward the apartment building's entrance. Joe draws his radio, yells to headquarters that they've been shot at, and informs them that they're now in pursuit of the suspect.

They had been told to wait, but two lives are at stake and enough lives have been wasted in this unnecessary war. As they reach the entrance, they hear screams...another body has collapsed on the pavement behind them.

Chapter Twenty-Eight

Supreme and his crew have made it into the kitchen of the apartment. Three of his men are badly injured, and one is dead in the center of the floor. The other one fell from the fire escape a few seconds ago.

Three dirty cops are splayed across the floor in various positions. Their bodies are motionless, and each one is laying in a deep puddle of blood.

Supreme goes to each dead cop, kicking their guns away from their bodies. A member of his team follows to pick them up.

Glancing up, Supreme speaks to his crew. "You all have your gloves on, right?" he asks.

They all nod their heads as they check on their injured friends. Two pick up their deceased friend from the floor and set his motionless body across the table.

Pointing to the bloody stains on the walls and the floor of the kitchen, Supreme growls. "Clean all of this up and get rid of these filthy ass cops." His boys know he means now.

The guy following him to retrieve the guns taps his shoulders. "What do you want us to do with them, Supreme?" he asks, pointing to the cops.

"Throw them out of the window. Fuck if I care...those worthless pieces of shit. Yeah, just throw them out the window," Supreme says. He then looks to his other compadre's. "And someone call one of our doctor friends to come out here and patch our crew up."

The members quickly get to following Supremes' orders. Two of them grab one of the cops from the floor. One is holding the arms and the other is holding the legs. They walk his body over to the open window and throw his limp body out just as if they were tossing out the trash.

The sound of his body splatting on the concrete below can be heard even from so high up.

Almost immediately after the sound of impact, people on the sidewalk begin screaming.

Supremes' guys go to hoist up the next dead cop. To their surprise, the cop jumps as soon as they grab him. He's injured badly, but not dead. Makes no difference to them. He's as good as dead anyway.

The evidence of pain and agony is heard in the cop's voice. "Ugh, please don't throw me out. I'm not dead. I'm alive, please?" The injured man begs for his life.

Supreme overhears this interesting last-ditch effort of life. He walks over to the dying man as they tote him toward the window. "So you're not dead, huh?" Supreme asks.

"No. Please don't do this. I'm not dead, and I'm a cop," he replies.

Supreme stops his men. "So you don't want to be killed, huh?" he asks, but doesn't wait for an answer. He beams his eyes deep into the depths of the man's soul. "But you killed my two friends, huh? And now you want me to spare your life because you're a cop?" He looks to his men. "Throw this bitch out," Supreme says.

The cop yells and screams as he tumbles to the pavement. His skull split like a watermelon on the impact.

The third cop is now moaning and apparently still alive, too, but that doesn't slow their pace. They sling his body out of the window just as quick as the first one.

Two men run in through the front door. "Supreme, they're shooting down on the fifth floor."

In Supremes' eyes, the glow of an anticipation to kill develops. He glances around the room once more. His injured crew members are being carried pass him. In his mind, he knows that the shit has finally hit the fan. It's too late to slow down, because there is no turning back.

Pointing to the water sprinklers on the ceiling, he starts giving orders. "Wrap them with some damp cloths and plastic, and then set this place on fire." Gripping his gun tightly, Supreme heads for the door. "Burn this building down!" he shouts. Seven men follow him out the door. "Tell everyone to leave! The building is burning down!"

Chapter Twenty-Nine

When Rell was shot in his hip area earlier, he didn't even realize where he was hit until he and Debbie made it to the fifth floor. They are already down the hall, and to the next stair well at the end of that hallway, before Rell really feels the wound. By that time his adrenaline slows down, and he catches his breath, he can barely move any further.   The fiery lead had burned straight through his flesh. Rell feels like his lower body is shutting down, but he refuses to let those cops kill him here.

Debbie has his arm resting on her shoulder. She sets him down on the stairs. "Don't move. Let me check your bullet wound," she says. Unbuckling his pants, she pulls the side of his pants down just enough to see the wound. "Oh dear, you're bleeding badly," she says. She uses the sleeve of her jacket to wipe the area around his wound. "Oh, thank God. You were hit, and it is bad, but it went straight through. It's a flesh wound."

Rell musters up a smile. "Oh, thank you Dr. Dee for your analysis."

She smiles as she retrieves a tampon from her purse. "Stay still," she says.

"Whoa, what are you doing?" Rell asks, suddenly becoming very uncomfortable.

"If it can stop a women's menstrual bleeding then it can stop your hip from bleeding, too." Opening the plastic wrap, she lets him know what to expect. "Okay, stay still. This is going to hurt a bit, but it will make sure that I don't lose you." She tries to calm his nerves, but his eyes are still the size of saucers.

She gently pushes the tampon into the bullet hole. Rell squirms and kicks a bit, but he doesn't make a sound. It hurts like hell, but he'd rather be in tremendous pain than to die before getting a chance to see those cops pay for what they did to the people he loved.

After the tampon is in place, Rell gets Debbie to cautiously peep through the vertical pane of glass on the stairway door to verify the location of the rogue cops.

She hurries back to him. "They're going from door to door, and they're only three doors from this stairway,"

Rell checks himself and his surroundings. He looks at the stairs. There's blood everywhere and it's his. There's nowhere left to hide. Going upstairs is too hard, so going down the next set of stairs is their only option.

He throws his arm around her neck and leans on her small frame for support. She assists him down. They're moving slowly, but no time is being wasted at all.

On the fourth floor, the two go from apartment to apartment, knocking on doors in hopes that someone will help. It seems like no one will even open their door, not that he can blame them after hearing all the gunshots.

After passing a few doors, an old lady from a couple doors back, opens her door. "Oh, dear. Can I help you children?" she asks, seeing they are in dire need of medical attention.

Her skin is soft and olive colored like her hair. She seems to be close to eighty years old, but she's agile like a sixty-year-old. She points at them with a shaky finger and repeats herself. "Excuse me, can I help you children?" she asks, again.

Debbie keeps Rell on her shoulder as she turns around. "Yes ma'am. May we use your phone to call for some help, please?" she asks the old lady.

The old lady looks to Rell. "Oh dear, is he hurt?"

"Yes ma'am, very badly, and I need to get him cleaned up, too." Debbie begins to feel a tiny sense of relief.

Giving a "come here" wave, the old lady summons them back to her apartment.

As soon as they make it inside, they see that the grandmother has already laid an old sheet on a chair.

Her little hand trembles. "Come on, dear. You can sit him here in this chair so that I can clean his wound." She bats her eyes; a flicker of a past life lights up her face. "I used to be a nurse, you know," the old lady says, grinning at the fond memory.

Rell gives a soft smile before asking for the phone. It hadn't taken a brain surgeon for them to figure out they had been tracked by Debbie's cell phone, so she pulled the battery out and threw it out a window when they were back in that first stairway.

Debbie finds the old woman's phone on an end table by the couch. " Rell," she says, "What's Supremes number?"

Rell aches to even think, let alone talk, but he gives her the number as best as he can.

The old lady looks up at the mention of Supremes' name. "Oh, you two know that nice young man?" she asks.

He groans, "Ugh, yes ma'am." Rolling his head back as the pounding pain hits him, he elaborates on their connection. "Yes ma'am, he's my longtime friend."

"Oh, wonderful!" she says, wiping the dried blood from his wound. "Hmm, so which one of you conjured up this idea to use a tampon in the bullet hole?" she asks. The old lady smiles. "I know wounds. I worked as a nurse for many years and wish more people had had the idea to do the same. It probably would've saved more lives," she says.

Debbie turns back, surprised and nervous. "I did, ma'am," she admits, barely above a whisper.

"This is a good idea," the old woman says. Debbie smiles a shy smile at the compliment.

Debbie waves her arm at Rell, "Rell, he's on the phone. It's Supreme."

Rell can barely hold his arm up to grab for the phone.

Debbie stretches the cord as far as it will go and hands the receiver to him.

"Hel. . . hello, Preme," he says.

Supreme asks him "what's wrong?"

"I've been shot." He becomes silent as he listens to his friend. "I think I'm on the fifth floor," he replies.

Debbie interrupts his conversation to correct him. "No. You're on the fourth floor." She turns to the old lady. "Ma'am, what's your door number?"

"It's 407, dear," the kind old lady says. Four-zero-seven. Four-zero-seven. Four-zero-seven. Debbie keeps repeating it to herself.

She takes the phone from Rell. "Supreme, this is Dee. Rell has been shot and he's losing a lot of blood, too." She gives Supreme the apartment number and ends the call after a few seconds. She looks back to Rell. "He said he's coming now, Rell. He's coming from the seventh floor."

The old nurse chimes in. "Honey, he's not bleeding too bad right now. The tampon worked as a good cork to the wound." The old lady is trying her best to reassure Debbie that everything is going to be okay.

Debbie smiles at the frail old woman. "I know, but I really need them to hurry." Setting the phone back on its receiver, Debbie thinks of such a silly request. "Oh yeah, ummmmm... do you have any shoes that I could borrow? It would be helpful if I could get out of these high-heeled boots," she asks the old lady.

"Um, yes, I do. My granddaughter has some clothes that she keeps here for whenever she comes into town." With her fragile finger, she points to a room just beyond the kitchen. "Just look into the closet in there. You're welcome to borrow anything you find," she tells Debbie.

Suddenly, someone is banging on the apartment door. "Miss Dodson," the voice yells, "the building is on fire! You have to leave!"

The old lady, who he now knows to be Miss Dodson, looks at Rell. "Oh dear, let me check the door. That's the nice young child from next door. He always checks on me from time to time."

Rell hasn't really heard a word she said. He just utters, "The buildings on fire?"

Debbie comes back into the room. "What's wrong?" she asks. She had changed shoes and put on an old sweater to cover up her tight black rock outfit. Before Rell can even answer her first question, she asks, "Did someone say fire?"

Rell seems grim. He just nods his head and continues to hold pressure on his wound.

The old lady returns from speaking to the neighbor's child at her door. "C'mon, children. We really do have to leave. The building is on fire."

Rell hurts badly, but he doesn't care. He wants out. He wants this to all be over. He wishes he would just wake up and find that everything had just been a terrible dream. He gets up and limps to the door to look through the peephole. He sees that everyone is indeed evacuating the building in an orderly fashion. People are even taking valuables with them as they exit the building. Apparently, it's not another con by the cops, which was the first thing that entered his mind when the kid had knocked on the old lady's door. Rell's not too good at trusting people lately.

He watches through the peephole for another few seconds and quickly notices everyone is leaving. Well, everyone but the two guys who are standing in the middle of the hallway, visually inspecting the people who are leaving their apartments to head for safety. Once again, Rell finds himself staring at Brewkowski with disgust. It's him and his fucked-up partner. "Dammit", Rell thinks. "I barely have time to plug a bullet wound with a tampon before they're right on my ass again," Rell sighs.

Turning back, his eyes find Debbie's. "Debbie. You and this sweet lady have to leave the building," he says, as calmly as he can.

Debbie doesn't back down this time. Rell's hurt, and she knows he won't be able to fend for himself very well. "Rell, I'm not leaving your side," she says, with a bit of attitude.

He shakes his head. His paled face starts to show a hint of fury, but then defeat. "Listen, Dee. I know what you think, but the only way we can stop these guys- or at least let the public know what's going on- is for one of us to make it." He grips his side as the sharp pain causes him to double over. "Ugh!!! I don't need to argue with you right now. I want you to escort this nice lady to the street, where it's safe for the both of you, and then you can contact the FBI or someone who will listen to us." Rell is done talking, and the look on his face tells Debbie that his suggestion is not up for further debate.

The old lady doesn't know exactly what's wrong, but she knows it has to be very serious for Rell to have a gun wound, for them to be so terrified, and for Rell to be asking the young woman to contact the FBI and not the police. Yes, something very bad and dangerous has happened and is still happening. She may be old, but her mind is still pretty quick. She knows she's surrounded by danger.

The old lady gently touches Debbie's arm. "Come with me, dear. We can make all of the proper calls once we get outside to a safe area." She tries to speak to Debbie in a motherly, caring tone. She knows the mindset that Debbie is in, and she doesn't want to play into the young woman's fear. Pulling Debbie toward the door, she tries to assert that the sooner they leave, the sooner they can call for help. "Debbie, I have a sweet friend in the building next door. She'll let us use her phone." She smiles and pats Debbie's hand, just as she would if Debbie were her own daughter.

Debbie still doesn't want to go, but she knows that there is no time to waste on arguing with Rell and Miss Dodson. She knows it's pointless to stand her ground at this point. There are some dangerous people on the other side of the door, waiting to kill them. She goes over and passionately kisses Rell. Silently, tears stream down their cheeks as they hug one another goodbye. Each one is hoping that it's not for the last time.

Rell pushes her away to the door.

Debbie and the old lady go to the door together. Debbie stops and looks back to Rell once more. She moves her lips, but no words come out. Only the movements of her lips say, "I love you."

Holding his hip to ease the pain, Rell watches the two of them as they ease out into the hall and close the door behind them.

After it closes, Rell pulls himself up, trying his best not to pass out from the pain as he limps to the door. He puts his eye against the peephole, wanting to watch the two women safely head for the exit route.

The two of them blend in well with everyone else. It's good that Debbie covered up her tight outfit or she would have definitely stood out like a sore thumb.

Oh no, Rell thinks. She's not paying attention. She's about to run into Brewkowski. She's headed right in his path. Rell holds his breath. Oh no, oh no, oh no.

Brewkowski looks right over her head. He didn't see her. For some reason, he's looking in

Rell's direction. Does Brewkowski know that was Debbie? Does he know Rell's location now?

Chapter Thirty

Trying their best to get through the thick crowd of people running down the stairs to exit the building, the two IAD detectives make sure they pay attention to every face that passes them.

Tom taps his partner's hip.

Big Joe doesn't have to turn to his side; he recognizes her, too. It's Debbie O'Brien and some old lady coming down the stairs, and they're about to run right into the pair of detectives.

The two detectives quickly turn around and act like they're trying to exit the building with the rest of the frightened crowd of people. However, they move a bit slower than the rest. They even split apart to allow everyone to pass between them.

A little girl stumbles as she passes between them. Luckily, Tom catches her in time by grabbing her coat.

It's hard for the detectives to stay on their feet when everyone is struggling and shoving to get between them.

Finally, Debbie and the old lady catch up with them. The detectives give them just enough room to barely squeeze between them. As soon as Debbie bumps into Big Joe, he rests his big hand on her tiny shoulder. At first, she freezes. Then, her fight or flight reaction sets in and she tries to jerk away from him. She quickly learns there's no use in trying to get away; Big Joe has a firm grip on her.

Big Joe speaks to in a super calm tone. "It's okay, Debbie. We're here to help you," he says.

She doesn't hear him and, despite his strong hold on her, continues to struggle for freedom.

Again Big Joe speaks, but this time with a firm voice. "Listen, we're here to help you."

Tom moves around the old lady. "That's right," Tom says, "We're here for you and Mr. Jacobs."

Once again, she tries to pull away from Big Joe's tight grip. "How do I know that you're not lying?" she asks. "Can you prove it? Can you prove that you're one of the good guys?"

Without hesitation, the two detectives pull out their wallets and display their badges. They know that, under the circumstances, even showing badges may not convince Debbie whose side they are on.

She takes one, and for some strange reason, the old lady grabs a badge, too. She sure is a quirky, frail, old bird, but if she may help convince Debbie that the detectives are genuine, then Brown and Riley are all for it.

Debbie holds Big Joe's wallet close enough to her face to see all of the important information in a blink of an eye. It's clear that he's an Internal Affairs agent of the New Jersey city police..

"Okay," she says, still with a lingering trace of doubt. "I believe you, but you have to hurry and follow me because he's stuck up stairs." Debbie points to the old lady. "In her apartment," she says. Now things are beginning to make a bit more sense to the detectives. They were wondering what connection there was between Rell, Debbie, and the old lady. Turns out, she was just at the wrong place at the wrong time. Or maybe, for Rell's sake, at the right place at the right time.

Detective Brown pulls Debbie back as she attempts to lead them upstairs. Big Joe speaks sharply. "No. We need you to go downstairs and meet the FBI when they get here. They're on their way. They will definitely need to debrief you."

Not wanting to, she gives in. "Okay, he's in her apartment," Debbie says again nodding towards the old lady. "She lives on the fourth floor in apartment four-o-seven." She sure wants to lead them there, but she knows they are professionals.

If they think she can help Rell more by waiting for the FBI, then that's what she's going to do.

Big Joe lets her and the old lady go. The two ladies immediately fall back into line with the crowd of people who are still rushing to safety.

The fiery Irish readies his grip around his pistol. "Well, big guy, we're only between the second and third floors. It'll be over in a few minutes." He takes a deep breath. "'You ready?" Tom asks.

Big Joe nods as he rechecks his clip.

Gun fire rings above from the fourth floor. Crowds of people are now frantically stumbling down the stairs to get to safety. Tom is knocked over.

Chapter Thirty-One

Brewkowski leans in from the frame of the door he just kicked in. The last member of Brewkowski's group is injured on the floor. Half of his friends' lower leg is basically gone; the only thing keeping the leg attached to its knee are a few tendons hanging, exposed like a slab of meat on display at a meat market.

He pleads for help as he reaches out for Brewkowski, but Brewkowski is a bit preoccupied with bigger issues and unable to help right now. Too much gun fire is coming their way.

Brewkowski continues to return fire. Brrrrrr! Brrrrrr! Brrrrrr! Although, he can't really see a true target, he shoots the AR-15 in the direction of his enemies.

Brewkowski's last remaining officer slowly crawls toward him. The bloody flab of flesh stretches as it drags the officer's lower leg behind it.

Brewkowski screams with anger and fear. "Come on, Jimmy_____!" He shoots his weapon. Brrrrr! Brrrrr! "Come on, _____! You can do it!" Brewkowski tries to give his friend the strength and courage to pull his severed leg just a tiny bit further.

As Brewkowski fights off the opposition, he thinks of the door that had all that blood on its door knob. That's where that bastard went, he deducts. Brewkowski can't help but to glance at the door with the bloody knob, because that's where he knows he has to go. He has to kill Terrell Jacobs and that whore who cheated on his best friend. If he doesn't, Brewkowski knows he'll live the rest of his life in prison, which definitely won't have a favorable outcome.

Brewkowski unleashes more rounds into the hallway. He yells, "Come on, Jimmy____! You can do it!" Squeezing his trigger – Brrrrr! Brrrrr! -, he says, "You're almost here!"

Brewkowski extends his arm out to help pull his friend the rest of the way. His pal doesn't reach back. Brewkowski glances down to the floor while still shooting and that's when he sees it. The back of his friend's head has been blown off. His friend's face is drowning in a puddle of his own blood. He gargles his last few breaths in that very spot.

A burst of desperation overtakes Brewkowski. He checks his waist for another clip, but there is nothing. He's about to run out of ammo. He and his crew weren't expecting their attack to have an outcome like this. They were supposed to come in and kill Rell and Debbie while the couple was having their little fuck fest in that apartment upstairs.

But now, everyone is dead but Brewkowski. Deep in his mind, he hopes that someone may come and save him; but, it doesn't take much more than common sense and deductive reasoning to know that if these guys who are shooting at him are down here, then the rest of his team must be dead. Otherwise, they would be trying to help him. Right?

He looks to his dying partner's body as it begins to have convulsions. Whatever small piece of life that had remained in his body after the shot to the head is now leaving for good. Not another second before– he's gone.

Brewkowski looks at the peephole on the bloody doorknob. He glares into the peephole's dark center like a hawk who just located a meal after being hungry all day. Suddenly, the shadow behind the door is gone. Whoever was there has moved, and Brewkowski is willing to bet that the shadow belongs to Terrell Jacobs.

Brewkowski's adrenaline goes into overdrive. He charges the door and kicks it in.

He can hear his attacker's charging toward him at full pace.

Out of nowhere, voices of the IAD are heard. "Drop your weapons. We're the police!"

Supremes team must be out of ammo, because they don't shoot their weapons. They run to the other stairway and escape.

Brewkowski sees a bloody handprint on the windowsill. He runs over to climb out.

As soon as he steps one foot out, someone yells, "It's over Brewkowski!"

Brewkowski freezes in his tracks and glances to Big Joe.

Big Joe holds his hands up. "Wait, it's over Brewkowski! You don't need another murder on your hands," he says.

A noise is heard from below. It's Terrell Jacobs. He fell from the fire escape as he tried to climb down. He fell into the garbage bin.

Brewkowski turns away from the two IAD detectives and climbs on to the fire escape to catch his star witness.

Chapter_Thirty-Two

Rell scrambles to get out of the dumpster. He's in great pain. In fact, it's the worst that he's ever experienced. His body aches with every movement. It feels like his tendons and muscles have been replaced with rusty steel cables and cracked joints.

He looks up and sees Brewkowski coming after him. He thinks, "Where is Supreme?" And then, it sinks in... another one of his friends is probably dead – by the hands of Brewkowski and his team of dirty cops.

Something overcomes Rell. Suddenly, he forgets about all of the physical pain that he feels, and he remembers all of the pain that his irresponsible self has inflicted upon his wife, children, and friends. Repeating the thought...

He looks back to Brewkowski as his anger builds. "I hurt everyone I love," Rell says to the world.

There's no more pain in his body. He forgets about all of that. He climbs from the dumpster and hides around the back, out of Brewkowski's sight.

Rell watches as Brewkowski climbs down the fire escape ladder as far as he can.

Rell takes off in Brewkowski's direction as soon as the dirty cop drops down from the ladder. Rell tackles him with all of his might, knocking Brewkowski's assault rifle and pistol away from him.

The two roll over several times as they tussle for their lives. They're both exhausted. They're both scared. And they both have everything on the line. One must die.

Rell immediately starts throwing upper cuts and short jabs to Brewkowski's midsection. Rell's keeping his chin low as he swings at Brewkowski with all his might.

Brewkowski has his arms wrapped around Rell's neck. His grip is super tight, and he refuses to let go. He keeps trying to twist his wrist from side to side as he locks tighter and tighter around Rell's neck.

Rell's jab is really weak because of his injuries. His body has been bruised and battered pretty badly. However, he's giving this beat down everything he has.

Rell's beginning to get light headed from the choke hold. He tries to wiggle his head out from under Brewkowski's thick arms. Rell can't unpin himself; he's too weak.

Brewkowski is trying to tear Rell's head from his shoulders. He wraps his legs around Rell's lower torso to maintain his death clutch.

Rell's vision is becoming blurry. He's beginning to lose consciousness. More fear meets his thoughts. He's getting weaker and weaker by the second.

Brewkowski grins as he chokes his victim. "Die like your bitch, nigger."

Rell becomes saucer-eyed with a mixture of anger, shock, and fear. Did he just say die? Like my...

Brewkowski's smile grows. "You know, Rell, I fucked your wife really good before I killed her. Oh, and did you know that she even claimed to have ovarian cancer? Her pussy was so tight; it definitely didn't seem like anything was wrong with any of her female parts. I could tell one thing though with that pussy being so tight- you sure didn't know what to do with all of that good ass." He laughs. "She died this morning," he tells Rell. Brewkowski tightens his grip even more. "Oh, and guess what?" he asks. Tightening his grip to its max. "She really had cancer, too," Brewkowski says, putting nails in the coffin of his confession to Rell.

Rell's eyes fill with tears of fire, then turn bloody red with rage. His veins fill with a burning desire for vengeance.

Like an explosion, Rell screams with a burst of murderous energy. "I'll kill you!!!" he says.

Turning his head as much as possible in Brewkowski's death grip, Rell bites his teeth deep into Brewkowski's thick, fleshy neck. He clamps down and pulls on the murdering cop's neck like a lion trying to tear through a water buffalo.

Brewkowski begins to scream in horror and pain. He can actually feel his skin ripping from this body.

He lets Rell go and crawls away to safety.

Stumbling to regain his footing, Rell searches for the assault rifle that he had knocked from Brewkowski when he initially rushed up at the fire escape ladder. His body is aching. His vision is blurred. His muscles are extremely weak. He's still losing blood from the bullet wound. He doesn't know if he's dizzy because of the bullet wound, or if it's because of the python-like choke hold that Brewkowski had had on him.

Brewkowski is still gripping his neck where he was bit as he scrambles to his feet, but he may be too late. He can see that Rell is already by the AR-15.

Bending over, Rell hears the two other cops coming down the fire escape. He knows that if he doesn't get his hands on this weapon, he will be killed on the spot. However, he'll get his vengeance on the man who raped and murdered his wife.

Rell almost falls as he reaches down for the weapon. His body wants to give up so badly, but Rell still manages to grab the AK without falling over, and planting his face on the pavement.

Tom and Big Joe both yell down from the fire escape. "Terrell Jacobs, drop that weapon."

Rell ignores them, and struggles to stand erect. Again, the IAD detectives yell. "Mr. Jacobs, we're here for you!" they say. They stop in their tracks right above him. "We know the whole story! You're not going to prison! We know that you were set up!" They holler down at Rell.

Rell aims the gun at Brewkowski's head.

Brewkowski uses his hands to block his head, as if they could actually stop the lead from hitting him.

Rell's throat is extremely dry, but he tries to speak anyway. "Hhhhh – he killed mmm-my wihhhfe." he says, thinking the detectives will now understand why he has to kill Brewkowski.

Big Joe and his partner can barely hear him, but Joe knows exactly what Rell has just said.

The big detective thinks of something that may be the only thing to possibly get Rell to put the gun down. "Listen, Mr. Jacobs. If you kill him, your children will lose both a mother and a father! You will die in prison and your children will have no one! They need you to be with them. They don't need you to die or go to prison!" Big Joe wants to jump down to the ground at this point, but he doesn't want to startle Brewkowski.

Detective Riley tries to reason with him, too. "Mr. Jacobs, please let us handle this. We don't want to have to shoot you! Please drop the weapon!"

Rell's hesitant, but he knows that these two cops are right. But wait – who are these cops? He thinks more. Maybe they're New York cops. Maybe that private detective tipped them off.

Using the last of his strength, Rell tosses the weapon towards the dumpster.

As soon as the rifle hits the ground a round goes off. Rell's eyes open with amazement, because it feels like a round hit him on the right side of his chest. He has no idea where the round came from. He looks down to his chest as he falls backward to the ground.

Big Joe and his partner watch in horror as their prime witness hits the pavement.

Without hesitation, they jump from the balcony. Before another round is fired, they land on top of Brewkowski. The impact knocks the gun from Brewkowski's hand.

Tom flips the dirty cop over and clamps the cuffs around his wrists.

Big Joe's sprung his ankle from the jump, but he forces himself up from the pavement. He hops and limps as he makes his way over to where Rell is crumpled on the ground. Blood is everywhere.

Several patrol cars screech their tires as they slam their brakes, blocking the ally entrances. A steady stream of officers come running from around the corner. Each is yelling the same directive. " Drop your weapons!" comes from all directions.

There's a marksman who has just set up behind one of the patrol cars. He already has Detective Brown's head in the crosshairs.

The swarm of officers are all wearing bulletproof vests with identifying department logos. Some of the vests have IAD or ATF, and other vests have the well-known FBI or NYPD prominently displayed in large visible letters. Every task force in the area is being represented at this one unfortunate place. Even Homeland Security is pulling up at the end of the ally. Looks like all bases have been covered - the law enforcement family is complete.

The IAD partners know this is not a game. They throw their weapons far away and place their hands behind their heads. At the same time, they both get down on their knees.

Big Joe cautiously yells out. "We're Jersey IAD! We need an ambulance! "

One of the FBI agents steps from the crowd of lawmen and points his finger at Big Joe and Tom. "Don't shoot! Don't shoot!", he commands the armed crowd. "These two are with us!" the agent says, still pointing at the IAD detectives. He starts walking toward them. "Do like they said," the agent continues, "get an ambulance out here!"

Rell coughs up some blood as he lay in the middle of the ally. He wonders if this is how helpless that cop felt the night he was shot in that New Jersey ally.

Rell can barely move his head, but he can tell that there are police everywhere. The swirling lights from the various official vehicles are reflecting from the building wall; their crackling radios echo inside of Rell's head, along with what seems to be a million footsteps.

Suddenly, the two cops that saved his life appear over him. The two of them seemed very concerned about his well-being before Brewkowski shot him, and obviously they still care now. Both IAD detectives kneel down beside him.

Tom rips his shirt open. "Don't worry, Mr. Jacobs. I'm going to try and slow your bleeding until the ambulance gets here," he says. Another officer brings Tom a towel. "I'm just going to apply a bit of pressure to slow the loss of blood," Tom says, making sure Rell knows they're trying to help him.

Big Joe leans in closer to Rell. "How do you feel, son? Can you speak?"

Rell's body is extremely weak. He wants to talk, but his throat is so dry that he can't. He opens his mouth, but nothing comes out. The fear of helplessness brings about more dread. Who would have thought that it would come to this?

It was only an affair. He didn't even want to have an affair. He just wanted the love that his wife, Sheila, wouldn't give him. He just wanted to be held by her soft, gentle touch. Not that it should be an excuse or justify his actions, but the whole time he was cheating on his wife in order to fulfill his needs that weren't being met at home, he didn't know that she had been diagnosed with ovarian cancer. She probably didn't know how to tell him. Sheila probably thought he would have left her.

And in the end, he betrayed her in every way. It's him who even caused her rape and subsequent murder.

The black officer shakes him a bit. "Stay with us, son. Don't fade out on us. We know you're tired and in unbelievable pain, but you must stay awake. Help should be here soon."

Rell's eyes become glassy. He doesn't even hurt that bad anymore, he thinks. His body feels like it weighs a ton. He can't even move a finger. He's starting to feel cold all over.

Tom takes off his coat and covers Rell's chest. "Don't worry, guy. Help is on the way. You have to make it for your children. They need you. Don't let this bastard, Brewkowski, get away with all that he did." Rell barely hears what Detective Riley is saying to him.

Rell's body begins to shake uncontrollably, just as Debbie comes into his view.

She's screaming with her hands over her mouth. She's horrified by how she sees Rell.

Rell is helpless. He has no control over what his body is doing. He can hear the ambulance making it to the scene. The paramedics are rushing to him.

His body is no longer heavy. He feels like he's weightless. He can't feel any more physical pain. He tells Debbie that he's sorry, but she can't hear a word he's saying.

The police are trying to pull her back.

Rell wonders who's going to contact Phillip's wife to tell her what to do with his and Sheila's children. The children will need to come to his funeral. Rell knows he's not going to make it.

The paramedics begin to connect wires and tubes to his body. They begin to talk with him, but he's unable to respond. They pick him up and slide him onto the gurney.

Rell's eyes are growing weaker and weaker. He can't hold them open any longer.

Someone screams, "We're losing him!"

It's Not A Game by Voll Greene & G's-Spot Publishing coming soon…

The Interview

Sophia: So Voll, it's been a while since our last interview. I see a lot has changed. I see that you're back on the east coast. How have you been?

Voll: Yes, I am finally back on the east coast and it feels so good to be here. I have been grinding a lot lately which keeps me in travel most of the time. However, you know I had to stop by to see my peoples.

Sophia: I see that your novel gave us a touch of reality on police brutality. How do you feel about what's going on in our society?

Voll: I dislike it totally. There are some who want to believe that people of color are deserving of harsh treatment, however, I beg to differ. I have dealt with corrupt police first hand, and it's not a good feeling when a split second could change your entire life.

Sophia: Would you elaborate on that please?

Voll: I will not make this about myself. However, it's bad when you're unable to count the amount of people you know that has had to deal with police abuse or brutality directly because the numbers are too high; you will lose count. Everyone can't just be complaining. There is a real issue there and it needs to be addressed. Across America people are calling for help. We have military service members who have been convicted of injuring or killing unarmed enemies in a war zone. Yet, in our own country unarmed people are getting murdered in their own communities and nothing happens. Something needs to change...

Sophia: I completely agree with you. Oh, and before I forget to say it. I'm sorry for the loss of your mother and brother. I know how close you were with them.

Voll: Thanks so much.

Sophia: I noticed that you pointed to the sky when you said, thanks. What is that about?

Voll: That's my way of just being grateful. My mother and brother were and are nothing but blessings to my family. I come from a big family and we're all blessed to have had them.

Sophia: If your mother was alive and well what do you think she would say about this masterpiece, if she had the opportunity to read it?

Voll: Masterpiece?

Sophia: Why are you blushing? I really like your work. I really love your first book. When are you going to publish that one?

Voll: "It's Not a Game," is coming out next so be on the look out. You know me, I don't sleep.

Sophia: Okay, the last two times that we met you were driving foreign cars that cost three hundred thousand dollars. Why are you driving American again?

Voll: I have changed. I fully support unions that support our people. When I purchase anything, I try to purchase from companies that have unions. Years ago, I didn't understand fully what it meant to support the working people. I can say today, I do now; without a shadow of a doubt.

Sophia: So, what is so special about the unions?

Voll: Unions are the voices of the people. We have overtime pay after 40 hours of work during a week because of unions. We have sick time, vacations, equal pay, health benefits, retirement benefits and competitive pay and many more things in place, all due to unions and similar groups fighting for the people. I support those that support me.

Sophia: What do you say to the people who complain about union dues?

Voll: I ask them to explain how can any nonprofit organization operate without some source of contributions? Unions provide legal teams and fair representation to all. Unions even fight for people that don't even realize that they are being fought for. The average person cannot afford a personal attorney. Therefore, unions usually ask for a one percent contribution. The numbers may vary depending on which union. However, I truly believe that it is a small price to pay to ensure equality.

Sophia: Many call you one of the realest authors to hit the scene in a long time. A lot of people are talking about your street credentials. How do you feel about that?

Voll: I only want to convey the real struggles of life. I have been through some difficult times, and I'm guessing that some like to read the work of those who can really relate to their struggle, feel their pain and understand their world. I can only be me. What you see is what you get.

Sophia: In your book "It's Not a Game" you highlight family abuse in that novel. Do you mind giving us a glimpse of that?

Voll: Well... this I can say: Many families have some level of abuse. Abuse comes in many forms. In my book that's due to be out very soon, I wanted to put it all on the table. In fact, writing that book was therapeutic for me. Writing that book allowed me to get a lot off of my chest, and I pray that it will help the next person do the same.

Sophia: Well, there you have it guys. Please go out and buy "Dead Man Standing" by Voll Greene. It's one of the hottest novels that I've read in a long time.

www.ingramcontent.com/pod-product-compliance
Lightning Source LLC
Chambersburg PA
CBHW070839250626
47159CB00003B/841